"Mel, you don't understand..."

Kerry laid a placatory hand on his arm, anxious to explain that she would never have agreed to go on holiday with Nick Albioni if she'd known he was married.

"You do me an injustice, Kerry," Mel told her dryly. "I understand very well how easy it is to be deceived by a beautiful face, but we can't argue about it now. Come along—it's time to leave."

Kerry silently followed him, still trying to come to terms with what she had learned about Nick, a man she trusted.

Mel paused before they left the building. "One other thing.... There are nearly two thousand miles and fourteen days before we reach Cairns, and I intend to watch you every step of the way. Put one foot wrong, break one company rule, be the cause of one complaint, and even the fact that you're Murray Davies's granddaughter won't save your hide!"

Angela Wells left the bustling world of media marketing and advertising to marry and start a family in a suburb of London. Writing started out as a hobby, and she uses backgrounds she knows well from her many travels for her books. Her ambitions, she says, in addition to writing many more romances, are to visit Australia, pilot a light aircraft and own a word-processing machine.

Books by Angela Wells

HARLEQUIN ROMANCE

2903—DESPERATE REMEDY
2921—FORTUNE'S FOOL
3006—STILL TEMPTATION
3054—RASH CONTRACT
3143—SUMMER'S PRIDE
3167—ENDLESS SUMMER

HARLEQUIN PRESENTS

1164—LOVE'S WRONGS
1181—ERRANT DAUGHTER

TORRID CONFLICT
Angela Wells

Harlequin Books

TORONTO • NEW YORK • LONDON
AMSTERDAM • PARIS • SYDNEY • HAMBURG
STOCKHOLM • ATHENS • TOKYO • MILAN
MADRID • WARSAW • BUDAPEST • AUCKLAND

Give me more love or disdain.
  The torrid or the frozen zone
Bring equal ease unto my pain
  The temperate affords me none

Thomas Carew.

Original hardcover edition published in 1991
by Mills & Boon Limited

ISBN 0-373-03246-3

Harlequin Romance first edition January 1993

TORRID CONFLICT

CHAPTER ONE

THE penalty was harsh, unwarranted and unfair! Kerry strode athletically along Sydney's George Street, her lithe body tense with umbrage, shoulders squared, round, positive chin lifted defiantly, hazel eyes narrowed against the strong winter sunshine which bathed the Harbour City from a sky of cerulean purity.

Of course Nick had been in the wrong. She would be the last person to deny that. Traffic laws were intended for the protection of life and health, and should be obeyed, but there were limits to how much a transgressor should be made to pay for his sins! Surely the three points' penalty on his licence was punishment enough for a simple and slight speed infringement? It wasn't as if he'd been driving recklessly or while drunk—just a little too fast. So it was nothing short of sadism for Mel McKinley to deprive him of his livelihood for two weeks.

She drew in a deep breath, savouring the sparkling air flavoured with the tang of the sea as the light wind lifted inward from the Pacific Ocean. Murray had felt the same way as she did, she was positive of it. When she had phoned Melbourne to make him privy to her outrage he had been most sympathetic to her point of view. It had only been his sense of propriety which had prevented him from raising the matter himself. During the seven months since she had left England to seek a reunion with her grandfather she had grown to understand and respect his rather reactionary attitudes.

'Although I still hold fifty per cent of the shares in Metline,' he had explained to her gently, 'they form a very small part of the McKinley operation as a whole—

7

certainly not enough to form any base from which to challenge the chairman's decision!'

'But I thought on a personal basis. . .' She'd allowed the sentence to wither to a stop. Perhaps on a personal basis there wasn't as much camaraderie between the two men as Murray had liked to claim. If Mel McKinley had truly felt a grain of friendship for her grandfather, surely he would have put in an appearance at the party Murray had thrown to celebrate his seventieth birthday, instead of pleading a heavy workload at the last moment? It wasn't as if the flight between Melbourne and Sydney was a long one by Australian standards. Although Murray had accepted his excuse on its face value, as far as she was concerned it had been a deliberate snub.

Murray had begged the suggestion, saying cheerfully enough, 'These things are always done better face to face than over the phone. Why don't you go and see him yourself and plead Nick's case, since you feel so strongly about it?'

Kerry paused for a moment, fishing into the pocket of her jacket to produce a small map. That was the office— right at the next turning and right again. Continuing her determined pace, neatly making her way through the morning rush of pedestrians, she decided that she'd been pessimistic in topping her light blue pebble-washed jeans and brushed cotton sweater with an outer garment, hardly anticipating a winter temperature of twenty degrees Celsius.

Ah, there it was! Stopping for a moment on the threshold of the building she had been seeking, she approved the window display of colourful posters surrounding a cut-out of a luxury coach bearing the trade name her grandfather had adopted over forty years previously—Metline—an acronym for Murrays Express Tours.

As the glass door opened smoothly beneath her touch she found herself in a pleasant soft-carpeted office with ample comfortable seating and a counter exhibiting a full panoply of enticing photographs.

'I should like to speak to Mr McKinley, please.' She spoke firmly as soon as the pretty blonde behind the counter raised her eyes from the VDU she was operating, not giving her a chance to speak first.

'I'm afraid that's impossible.' The girl smiled with professional charm. 'He's on the phone at the moment and he's already running late for an appointment. If you'll let me know what the problem is, I'm sure I can help.'

'And I'm sure you can't!' Kerry smiled to take the sting from her reply. 'It's a personal matter. He'll spare me a few moments when he knows who I am.'

'Oh!' The blonde looked a little uncertain, as Kerry suppressed a smile. What was the other girl thinking—that she was Mel McKinley's girlfriend, newly arrived from Perth intent on orchestrating a loving reunion? Murray had already told her about the rumours circulating through the company about the cooling-off of Mel McKinley's long-standing relationship with Belinda Fraser, the darling of Perth society. If the man was as unfeeling and didactic as his treatment of Nick implied, then the unknown Belinda had all her sympathy!

'If you'll give me your name I'll ring through to his office—but he really is pushed for time,' the receptionist offered tactfully, clearly not wishing to stand in the way of true love.

'Don't bother!' Kerry had caught the quick upward glance almost at the same time as she had seen the staircase leading in the same direction at the back of the counter. 'This won't take a moment!'

Confidently she made for the stairs, turning a deaf ear to the blonde's wail of protest. She was Kerry Davies, granddaughter of the founder of Metline, wasn't she? And she wasn't going to be fobbed off with excuses contrived for lesser mortals. Murray and Mel McKinley

were partners, after all, and although her grandfather
held only nominal shares in McKinley's Tours, as far as
Metline was concerned they were on an equal footing!

There were three doors at the top of the stairs, but she
was in little doubt as to which one was her target.

'It's your responsibility to ensure that such staffing
problems don't arise!' Impatience riddled the taut tones
that echoed from the only half-open one. 'I'm sorry, but
my decision stands. If you can improve your organis-
ational set-up we might consider you again for the next
season, but for the time being I'm ending our arrange-
ment on the grounds of breach of contract!'

Not the best of moments for her to have chosen—but
time was at a premium. Kerry grimaced to herself as she
heard the receiver replaced firmly on its rest, pushing
the door open after a preliminary knock and advancing
into the room, hoping she looked dignified and
businesslike.

'Mr McKinley. . .' She smiled with more enthusiasm
than she felt as a pair of light grey eyes set in a
surprisingly attractive face glared at her with barely
hidden hostility. 'I'd like to introduce myself——'

'Not now, sweetheart.' He brushed her presence aside
with the careless indifference one applied to the flies in
summer, as he grabbed at the leather jacket flung lazily
over the back of his chair and shrugged his powerful
shoulders into its expensive lining.

'You don't understand——' she began again a little
desperately as he swept up a pile of papers lying on his
desk, stuffing them into a manila folder while he muttered beneath his breath.

'No—*you* don't understand, sweetheart!' It was almost
a bark as he repeated the endearment with that particular
intonation which turned it into a derogatory label. 'I've
got about five minutes to catch the Manly hydrofoil so,
whatever it is you're selling, I'm not interested!' A quick
flick of his cold eyes assessed her from crown to toe,

with a chilling competency. 'Call in the same time tomorrow if you like, and I might reconsider—if the price is right!'

'Now you're being insulting!' Kerry's eyes sparkled with a controlled anger. There was little point in losing her temper when she needed his goodwill, but she was darned if she'd allow him to treat her so dismissively! 'If you'd just let me explain. . .'

But she was wasting her time, being forced to take a small step backwards as he brushed past her to open the door fully, indicating with a brisk nod of his head that she was to precede him from the room.

'Downstairs!' he ordered curtly as she hesitated on the threshold, giving her no option but to obey him. Clearly there was no point in pursuing her quest at that moment. She needed time to give a reasoned argument, and ideally an environment where she could count on receiving his undivided attention.

'Mr McKinley,' she persisted desperately as she allowed him to usher her out of the premises into the street. 'I really do need to talk to you urgently. Tomorrow will be too late!' He'd already started out at a mean pace towards Circular Quay, and she found herself having to jog-trot to keep up with him as his long legs ate up the metres. 'Are you free at all this afternoon?'

'No.' They'd reached the busy road intersection in front of the Quay where the heavy traffic demanded they wait for the lights to change in their favour, and he glanced at his watch as he made the terse reply before turning his head to frown at the steady stream of cars, presenting his profile to Kerry's anxious gaze.

Uncompromising, she thought despairingly, for the first time beginning to doubt the success of her self-imposed mission. Everything about that strong-boned face declared him a tyrant. Everything from the broad, impatiently lined forehead, through the high-bridged, jutting nose with its surprisingly delicately chiselled, flaring nostrils and the long, sweeping curve of his top lip to the stubborn fullness of the lower one, above a chin of unremitting squareness made all the more formidable by the presence of a slight but definite cleft at its point.

But I have to admit your persistence intrigues me. . .'

Unexpectedly Kerry found herself subjected to a concentrated stare from the eyes she had dismissed as 'cold' in the office. Now their grey clarity was warmed by what could only be amusement at her perseverance, and she found herself reassessing her earlier verdict. Outlined by dark lashes beneath twin bars of straight brows, they appeared to glow with an interest which momentarily set her back on her heels.

'Ten minutes of your time would be enough!' she responded eagerly as she saw the lights begin to change, determined to retain her optimism until the last possible moment.

'Tonight, then.' He returned peremptorily. 'Meet me in the Park Lounge of the Menzies Hotel at eight, and I'll buy you dinner.'

'Oh! But I. . .' Surprise had put her off her guard, and he was already a couple of metres ahead of her as the lights changed and he strode out through the crowd towards his destination, as she found herself unable to catch up with him.

Damn the man! This wasn't what she'd wanted at all! And eight o'clock! Surely it would be too late then to alter tomorrow's schedules even if she was successful in putting over her point of view? On the other hand, from what she already knew, as well as from what she'd just seen, Mel McKinley wasn't the kind of man to let a small item like lack of hours defeat him from his purpose. She sensed he was of that breed of men who accepted power as their natural due and wielded it with a casual efficiency that suggested the idea that it might be challenged had never occurred to them.

Kerry sighed as she admitted to herself that she would have to keep the appointment for Nick's sake. . . And the wretched man hadn't even waited to hear her decision! Drawing in a deep, refreshing breath, she made a conscious effort to relax her taut muscles, surprised to find that she felt as agitated as if she'd been in a physical fight.

Beginning to walk along the broad, flowerbed-lined pathway towards the Ocean Terminal, she started to plan the intervening time, determined to make the most of what was going to be her last day in Sydney for several weeks. As the warm sunshine caressed her face she found her normal good humour surfacing. At least Mel McKinley wasn't all that infallible! She hoped with all her heart that he was feeling uncomfortably hot beneath his smart leather jacket!

Subsiding on one of the many public benches, she considered the many options open to her. Murray's suggestion that she took a break to sightsee in New South Wales's capital city before resuming her duties had been a welcome one, although she felt a little guilty that she was receiving preferential treatment over her colleagues. Still, Murray had insisted, and she supposed the circumstances were unusual enough to merit her accepting his using his influence with the operations manager to smooth her path.

Not many Australians knew as little of their homeland as she! Born in Melbourne twenty-two years previously, she'd left the continent for England with her mother just before her second birthday, when Louise Davies, homesick and mourning the death of her young husband in Vietnam, had fled from her father-in-law's house to find sanctuary with her own flesh and blood.

As ever when she thought of the father she had never seen, Kerry experienced a stab of desolation. Warren and Louise's marriage had been a Romeo-and-Juliet affair—and had ended just as disastrously, except in this case her mother had suffered the torture of having to go on living without the young Australian who had won her heart and married her within a month of their first meeting.

Murray, her mother had confided to her when she was old enough to understand, had opposed both his only son's joining the army and his marriage at such short notice. Nevertheless he had opened his house to the young, pregnant widow and offered her every material comfort.

It hadn't been enough. Louise had needed affection, and that had been something that Murray, in his own bereavement, had been unable to offer.

Closing her eyes, Kerry leaned back on the bench, offering her face to the kiss of the sun. Louise was warm and emotional, and it had been only natural that the limitless love she had bestowed on her daughter should have made Kerry feel protective towards her, unwilling to leave her to uncover her roots halfway across the world. Then an astounding thing had happened. Louise, at the age of forty-four, had fallen in love again, with a man who could offer her all the financial and emotional security she needed, and she, Kerry, had finally felt free to take a break from her job as a trainee in hotel management to discover the land of her birth.

It had always been her ambition from the days she had saved a portion of her pocket-money towards the fare. That sum had been augmented considerably from her latter earnings, and it had been with a glowing inner excitement that she had booked her flight, the most precious item among her luggage being the photograph of Warren Davies which had enjoyed place of honour on her bedside table for the past two decades.

Although her mother hadn't kept in touch with her father-in-law, Murray had been easy to locate, through the offices of Metline. Despite the fact that her grand-father had reached retirement age and sold out fifty per cent of his shares in the coach excursion company to McKinley's, taking no active part in the company's affairs now, he still retained a seat on the board and a place in the hearts of his long-serving staff!

Kerry sighed reflectively, recalling the warmth of his greeting and the hospitality he had offered her. She'd been tense and a little scared the day she'd presented herself on his Melbourne doorstep, prepared to beat a hasty retreat if she'd been met with cynicism or suspicion. In fact, Murray had welcomed her quite literally with open arms and, if she hadn't been adamant that she wanted to use her own resources to discover the land of her birth, would have been prepared to lavish on her a small fortune!

Well, this wouldn't do! Enchanted by the harbour, Kerry knew she could spend the whole day watching the ferries and pleasure-boats plying their trade, unless she made the effort to discover new pleasures. She rose determinedly to her feet, referring to her mental agenda. There was still the Darling Harbour development to explore, and a ride on Sydney's new mono-rail which swept above the city streets was a must! Nicknamed the 'monofail' by the irreverent Sydneysiders because of early teething troubles, it remained an experience that she was determined to enjoy!

After that she would buy sandwiches and eat them in the open air of Hyde Park, watching the giant chess game that was always in progress. That would leave her the afternoon to window shop at the Centrepoint complex, with a break for a cup of coffee and a slice of cheesecake at David Jones—the Sydney equivalent of Harrods.

She started back towards George Street with a brisk, swinging gait, acknowledging inwardly that if she wanted to keep her trim figure she would have to be wary of a culture where even something as calorie-laden as baked cheesecake was inevitably served accompanied with an

ample helping of whipped double cream liberally decor-
ated with strawberries and slices of kiwi fruit!

It was intensely annoying that she hadn't been able to
speak to Mel McKinley first thing. Mentally she
shrugged her irritation away. She wouldn't let her disappointment spoil the day ahead, although something
told her that she was going to have her work cut out to
make the chief executive of McKinley's sympathetic to
her point of view! After all, Murray had warned her
that, since his father's death two years previously in a
yachting accident, Mel McKinley had acted out the new-
broom theory with all the verve and enthusiasm of his
thirty years.

Despite the shadow hanging over her, Kerry's day
went very much to plan, and it was with a sigh of relief
that she found a seat in one of the city's double-decker
underground trains for the short ride to the suburb
where Metline kept four units available for any of their
staff in transit.

Heavens! How her feet ached! But she'd only have
time for a quick shower and change of clothes before
having to come all the way back again to the city centre
to keep her appointment, especially as she intended to
arrive at the rendezvous early, in the hope of catching
the elusive Mr McKinley before the arranged time. As
for dinner—well, he could eat that alone. It was business
she wanted to discuss, and that was something she had
no intention of mixing with pleasure. His, that was, not
hers. Frankly, she could think of nothing less pleasurable
than having to endure a meal eaten opposite that aggress-
ive countenance!

It was just past seven when she turned into Carrington
Street and made her way towards the Menzies, mounting
the steps and smiling at the attendant who came quickly
to open the glass doors for her. She'd dressed smartly for
the evening in one of the dresses she'd brought with her

from London. Dark violet, long-sleeved and straight-skirted with a fashionable width of shoulder still popular, its deep 'V' neckline showing to advantage her flawless creamy skin, while the depth of colour enhanced the gleaming red-gold of her naturally curly hair which hung in a carefully tamed curtain against her neck and shoulders.

The Park Lounge was on the first floor. Looking around with the avid interest which was part of her character, Kerry approved of its traditional, gentleman's-club-type comfort. Strange, but she'd assumed that the McKinley man would have preferred something snazzy—all glass and chrome and plastic. It seemed she had done him an injustice. The lounge was nearly empty, and certainly there was no sign of the man she'd come to meet. Selecting a table by the window, she ordered a coffee and prepared to wait. It was already dark but it was pleasant sitting there, glancing out of the window from time to time to enjoy the sight of the trees in the gardens opposite, their branches illuminated by the streetlights, moving slightly in the breeze.

Fascinated by the movement of the evening crowds and the regular passage of the single-decker buses from their terminus below her, Kerry almost missed him. Some inner sense must have made her turn her eyes from the window and glance towards the entrance to the dining-room just as Mel McKinley emerged from it.

'Mr McKinley!' She was instantly on her feet, advancing across the soft carpet towards him.

'Miss X!' He returned her greeting with mocking enthusiasm, ostentatiously looking at the businesslike watch which encircled his strong wrist. 'Either you're working on a different time zone from the rest of us, or you're unusually eager to see me again. If it's the former, then you must allow me to correct you. If the latter—well, I have to admit to being flattered.'

His smile was patronising, drawing out her resentment with the efficiency of a hot poultice.

'Such wit!' Her generous mouth aped an admiring smile. 'I've never agreed with that old adage about sarcasm, have you?' Let him draw his own conclusions if he was erudite enough.

Apparently he was, because his glance sharpened as he allowed himself the luxury of surveying her with minute attention to detail, as if she had applied for the job of a photographer's model and he was the man behind the camera.

Kerry's breath hissed in between her teeth at the frank appraisal to which she was being subjected.

'When you've finished. . .' Her tongue stuck on the word 'leering'. Partly because if she was honest she would have to admit there'd been no sexual innuendo in that encompassing gaze, but mostly because she needed a favour from him, and using provocative verbs was not going to dispose him to grant it. What was needed now before she blew the whole thing was a strategic withdrawal.

'Ah, but that's just it.' He contemplated her with a slight smile playing about his surprisingly sensuous mouth. 'I haven't nearly finished my preparations for the evening. Didn't anyone tell you that while punctuality is the courtesy of kings, arriving too early can be as inconvenient to your host as arriving too late?'

There was no way Kerry could stop the colour mounting in her cheeks at his mild admonition, but she'd been engineered into a position that was none of her choosing, and the sooner she disillusioned this big-headed ape the better!

'The whole point *is*, Mr McKinley,' she told him frostily, 'that I don't regard this as a social engagement. My name is Kerry Davies, my grandfather is Murray Davies, and I'm here on business. I have no desire to be wined or dined. I want fifteen minutes of your time, that's all.'

'Ah, so you're the prodigal granddaughter.' He was neither shocked nor dismayed, if his faintly amused expression was anything to go by. 'What am I supposed to do? Stand to attention or genuflect?'

'I wouldn't know,' she returned sweetly. 'I'm afraid I'm not up to date with all your quaint colonial customs.'

For the first time she dragged her eyes from his commanding face, sweeping their glance with deliberate disdain over his body. How on earth had Murray allowed himself to be taken in by this maverick to the extent of regarding him as a friend?

'For instance, where I come from it's customary for a gentleman to wear something a little more formal when he's invited a lady to dinner.'

Condescendingly her eyes dwelt on the disreputable jeans which clung to his disturbingly well-muscled legs before lifting to contemplate the colourful sweatshirt, proclaiming him a survivor of some long since departed cyclone, which clung to a frame every bit as powerful as she had first assessed.

'Even if she doesn't intend to accept his offer?' He was enjoying himself at her expense, and it infuriated her.

'Oh, so you're used to being turned down?' Kerry lifted well-shaped brows above hazel eyes which sparkled with the light of battle. 'How very well-adjusted of you to admit it. Most men——'

'Most men wouldn't be prepared to make time after the end of a tiring and frustrating day to entertain an unexpected intruder with a problem on her mind!' he interrupted tersely. 'And, for the record, one of our quaint colonial customs is to judge an individual on his own merits—not on his family tree! And now, if you'll excuse me. . .'

'No, please, Mr McKinley. . .' Seeing all her hopes

fading, Kerry placed an anxious hand on his upper arm
as he would have turned away, swallowing in embarrassment as she felt the muscle beneath her grasp tighten.
'Won't you at least listen to what I have to say?'

'I suppose it's the least I can do for Murray.'

Kerry flinched at his unwilling agreement as he sighed
with exaggerated weariness.

'OK. As I said—dinner at eight. Order yourself a
drink and put it on my bill.'

Stubborn wasn't the word for him! A wave of irritation
swept over Kerry as he moved away from her, heading
for the stairs which would take him to the ground floor.

'Look—ten minutes—and then you can have the rest
of the evening to yourself—or with a guest of your own
choosing rather than one thrust on you.' She had to
almost run to keep pace with him. 'I've got to be up
early in the morning and. . .'

'Suit yourself.' He shrugged with disarming pleasant-
ness. 'Have your say now if you must, sweetheart, but
you'll forgive me if I continue with my interrupted
programme, won't you?'

It was better than nothing. Kerry felt a glow of
satisfaction at having won her point as she arrived beside
him in the foyer. Even if he was checking up on his
phone calls and post she could begin her petition on
Nick's behalf.

'It's about Nick Albioni,' she started enthusiastically.
'He was scheduled to take the Tropical Queensland tour
leaving Sydney tomorrow.'

'Uh-huh.' The grunt was hardly encouraging, but at
least it proved he was listening as they reached a door at
the end of a short corridor and, pushing it open, he
indicated she precede him.

'Oh!' She stopped in total surprise as she found herself
standing on a short flight of steps which led down to a
fair-sized indoor swimming-pool.

CHAPTER TWO

THE room was deserted, smart loungers abandoned beneath glowing lights, a pile of white towels stacked temptingly on a counter, a spa-bath bubbling at one end of the pool as a thin layer of warm, damp air caught at Kerry's throat.

'You were saying?' Mel McKinley prompted, having passed her to stand on the green mock-grass surroundings, and beginning to tug at his sweatshirt.

Amazement and the futility of addressing someone whose head was enveloped in stretch-cotton held Kerry's tongue silent. Pectoral muscles expanded as strong arms lifted over the dark head with its golden highlights and the shirt was abandoned, casually draped over the seat of one of the loungers.

Disreputable trainers were toe-heeled off, exposing well-shaped feet while capable fingers lifted to the snap-fastening of his jeans. Fascinated, Kerry watched the impromptu strip-tease, still at a loss for words as the zip rasped downwards and firm hands peeled the garment away from his thighs, revealing skin as deeply tanned as his shoulders, but covered in a soft fuzz of golden hair.

Silently she continued her observation as, hopping on one foot, her would-be host extricated one leg from the binding garment before kicking it with precise aim to join his discarded shirt.

He had undressed as if she hadn't been there, removing his clothes with a peculiar masculine efficiency that, graceless in itself, still had the power to catch at her throat—or was it the humid atmosphere of the pool-room which was making it difficult for her to breathe? The very unseductiveness of his actions was surely a challenge to her presence there? Not that there was anything intrinsically wrong in his stripping down to the neat bathing trunks which covered his loins with acceptable modesty, so why did she get this strange feeling that he hoped to discomfit her?

Totally confident with his body—and why not? Kerry asked herself with grudging acknowledgement that she was witnessing a prime example of the mature male anatomy at its physical peak—he took the necessary few steps to bring him to the pool's edge at its deepest point and, obeying the signs which forbade jumping or diving, merely stepped off the edge to disappear momentarily from her sight with a moderate displacement of water.

What was she meant to do? Give up her quest in disgust? Sit admiringly on the side waiting for him to emerge? Clearly there was no future in attempting to address herself to someone whose head was partially submerged in water, as he effected an economical crawl from one end of the pool to the other and then back again.

'That feels better!' He'd chosen the deep end of the pool for his exit from the water, disdaining the pool ladder, to heave himself out of the pool by the sheer muscular strength of his arms. 'There's nothing like a few lengths to refresh you after a heavy day.'

'I'm so glad you found it therapeutic,' Kerry murmured ironically. Having decided not to react in any overt way to his behaviour, she'd helped herself to one of the white pool towels and, approaching, offered it to him.

'Thanks.' He stood there smiling, water streaming off him, as her sensitive nostrils absorbed the smell of chlorine mixed with an evocative trace of warm, clean male—the impact on her senses being so strong that she took a step backwards, away from him. 'I'll just shower away the traces of disinfectant and then I'll be with you.'

With the towel slung round his neck he stooped

slightly to collect his discarded clothes before disappearing in the direction of a sign reading 'Men's changing room'.

He was certainly quick, she admitted, when he was back at her side within a few minutes, fully dressed, hair slicked back and his damp bathing trunks screwed up in one mean hand.

Consulting the watch which had never left his wrist, he nodded his head with brisk satisfaction. 'By my reckoning I have time to put on something a little less casual and still keep our arranged date with ten minutes in hand. So I suggest you go back to the Park Lounge, order yourself an aperitif on my account, and wait for me to join you as originally arranged. Or——' he subjected her to the full battery of his light eyes, which gleamed with a lustre that had nothing to do with the shower he'd just taken '——would you prefer to come up with me to my room and I'll order something from Room Service? The choice is yours.'

It had always been his intention that she should dine with him, she recognised with reluctant admiration for his tenacity. But why?

'Because I've only been in Sydney for two weeks, and I've been too busy to get my social life organised. . .and because I find it amusing to listen to your tight little vowels.'

Colour flooded Kerry's face as he picked up her silent question and answered it without embarrassment, as if telepathic communication were the most natural thing in the world.

'Well?' Brows lifted, he awaited her answer.

There was only one she could give him, and she delivered it with the cool frostiness of an English February morning.

'I'll see you in the lounge.'

* * *

'So what's the problem?'

Lifting the bottle of Hunter Valley Chardonnay from
its ice-bucket beside him, her table companion topped
up Kerry's glass.

True to his word, Mel McKinley had rejoined her ten
minutes before their agreed meeting-time, dressed in a
pale mushroom-coloured silk shirt, short-sleeved with a
conservative dark brown tie loosely knotted at the neck,
above pale oatmeal, fashionably tailored trousers, and
led her into the restaurant where he had reserved a table.

Since it had become abundantly clear to her that he
had no intention of listening to her a moment before he
deemed the time right, Kerry had forced herself to hold
her tongue. Dislike it as she did, there was no point in
alienating him before she'd even begun to make her
point. He had her precisely where he wanted her, knew
it, and was taking a supercilious, typically masculine
pleasure in the fact.

Given permission to speak, Kerry found herself temporarily at a loss for words, all her carefully prepared
phrases deserting her beneath the disconcerting stare
levelled at her. Being the sole object of Mel McKinley's
attention was as disturbing as being ignored by him, she
realised, her voice muscles tightening in unexpected
tension. Murray's affectionate summation of this man's
character as resourceful, dominant and ambitious had
failed to prepare her adequately for the reality of his
powerful presence—probably because her grandfather
had also likened him with wistful recollection to his own
son Warren! Surely her mother—sweet-natured, docile
Louise—would never have fallen for such abrasive
sensuality?

'I feel it only fair to warn you that I don't take personal
responsibility for my employees' love-lives—so if Nick
Albioni's made you pregnant——'

'Mr McKinley! I resent your inference!' Eyes ablaze
with anger as the outrageous suggestion catapulted her

back to her present quandary, Kerry pushed her seat
back preparatory to rising. One slim hand rested on the
table, the other scrabbled on the floor beneath her chair,
searching for her handbag. The man was impossible! He
couldn't have made it plainer that she was wasting her
time even attempting to have a sensible conversation
with him.

'Then I apologise,' he said mildly. 'Come on, Kerry,
drop the injured innocence act. It was a natural conclusion, since you appear to be experiencing such difficulty in expressing yourself, and apparently Murray
hasn't been able to pull your chestnuts out of the fire for
you, or you wouldn't be here. Finish your oysters.'

Her hand resting on the tablecloth was touched gently,
and she withdrew it instantly as if it had been scalded.

'I don't recollect asking you to call me by my Christian
name.' She temporised, knowing she was reinforcing all
the worst impressions he had formed about her. Tight
little vowels indeed! Perhaps her accent was slightly
more clipped than his slower form of speech, but it was
none the worse for that. She glowered across the table at
him, torn between marching out in umbrage or staying
and finishing her meal as he'd suggested.

The oysters were delicious. Since arriving in Australia
she had made a point of eating the specialities of the
locality, delighting particularly in the seafood—the succulent crayfish rather off-puttingly called Balmain bugs
and the tender, tasty Sydney rock oysters having become
particular favourites. To abandon her meal now might
feed her pride, but it would hardly assuage her hunger
pangs, and it certainly wouldn't further Nick's cause.

'Oh, we're a very informal people,' he responded
easily, apparently in no way offended by her sharpness.
'I thought you might prefer being called by your given
name rather than being called "sport" or "mate".'

His wicked eyes were deriding her as she pulled her
chair towards the table and lifted her fork as instructed,

aware that he was watching her benignly as she took a mouthful.

'That's better,' he approved as she swallowed, following the action by taking a sip of the dry white wine, with its delicious after-taste of honey and the tang of the oak barrels in which it was matured. 'Now, you were going to say?'

'That I think you have been too harsh in suspending Nick just because he got a private speeding conviction.' There, it was out, although she hadn't intended to put her point so baldly.

'Is that all?' He managed to look surprised. 'Well, you're entitled to your opinion, of course, but you seem to have gone to a lot of trouble to make it known to me. I'll try to remember it if anyone asks me about your feelings.' He cut into his steak with evident enjoyment, releasing her from his irreverent regard.

'I was hoping you might reconsider your—your *arbitrary* judgement!' she said between her teeth. The wretch! He was deliberately baiting her. 'Isn't it enough for you that he's been fined and lost three points against his licence?'

'No.' He faced her squarely, and now there was no lurking amusement in the crystal grey of his irises or the sharp black pupils. 'When Nick Albioni is behind the wheel of one of my coaches he holds the lives of forty or so people in his hands. The coaches are heavy, the Pacific Highway—despite the charisma of its name—is more often than not a narrow and dangerous road. Sometimes you may hear it referred to as the Crystal Highway—not because it runs beside the glistening ocean, but because at times it sparkles with the shattered glass of careless drivers' windscreens!'

'Nick would never speed behind the wheel of a coach. . .'

'Not one of mine, certainly,' he agreed smugly. 'Did

you know that whatever the statutory penalty for speed-ing, a coach driver's penalty is automatically doubled because he has put other people's lives at risk?'

Exasperated, Kerry let out her breath in a sigh of indignation.

'And I suppose *you've* never put your foot down a bit too hard?' she asked sarcastically.

'Not on the pedal of a car,' he agreed with infuriating complacence. 'He can count himself lucky that he's still got a job with McKinleys. A fortnight without pay to think about his sins won't hurt his pocket as much as his pride. If it hadn't been for the intervention of the operations manager on his behalf he would have been out on his ear as far as I'm concerned.'

'Well, at least you make no claims for exercising compassion.' Kerry contrived to appear pitying. 'I just hope that you never need clemency from anyone and, for the record, the company he works for is Metline not McKinleys.'

'Only out of courtesy to your grandfather's wishes.' His gaze narrowed thoughtfully. 'I don't know how much you know about the situation, but Metline was in a pretty bad way when McKinleys came on the scene five years ago. It had good established routes on the east coast, but the rolling stock needed renewing, the level of service needed improvement, and a good publicity cam-paign to continue competing with its rivals was essential. If McKinleys hadn't been interested in buying the goodwill, Metline would have been out of business by now, and Murray probably bankrupt as well.'

It was true. Her grandfather had been quite frank about his position.

'Now, if I'd still had a son to inherit the business,' he had explained sadly, 'there would have been an incen-tive, but as it was. . .'

'And you were the White Knight riding to the rescue across the red desert from Perth to save an old man's pride and ensure his continuing comfort into a lonely old age?'

'You give me far too much credit, my dear Kerry.' He smoothly ignored her sarcasm. 'If you insist on speaking in market terms, then you must cast me as a dawn raider pouncing on the vulnerable and consuming it, to grow fat on the proceeds without a care for casualties.'

'So you have no pretensions about your motives.' Her curious gaze rested on the thick dark brown hair that waved disarmingly across the edge of his forehead, breaking the symmetry of the broad expanse, softening it.

Yet, despite his harsh admission, the fact remained that he had made no argument against the east coast operation's continuing under the name Murray had given it, even after he had taken over full control of McKinleys on his father's death, although surely it would have been better from a corporate point of view to function under one nationally known name?

'Very few.' He answered her allegation, a slight smile twisting his firm mouth as if acknowledging a compliment. 'I was raised on the text "To thine own self be true. . ."'

'Shakespeare?' Kerry couldn't curb the surprise in her voice, and was rewarded by a narrowing of his gaze and a tightening of his formidable jaw.

'That amazes you? We do have schools and universities in the Antipodes, you know.'

'Of course I know!' Kerry retorted hotly, stung by his contempt. 'I don't know why you should assume anything else. I'm Australian by birth and blood even though it's the first time I've been able to come back here. Ever since our first meeting you've been trying to put me down, and to be honest I'm getting fed up with it! What is it with you? Does my accent offend you? Have you got something against women with red hair? Or perhaps it's just the female gender generally you dislike?'

She was shaking with the effort needed to control her voice to a low tone so as not to make a scene in the busy restaurant, and furious with herself for allowing him to needle her to such a degree that she'd forsaken the tenuous hold on her temper.

'Now you're angry.' Mel stated the obvious with such satisfaction that her hand itched to wipe the smug smile from his face. 'Have some more wine.' He refilled her glass as she stared stonily at the tablecloth. 'Your hair and your accent are quite delightful, and I can assure you my appetite and predilection for the female sex can be well attested to, although naturally I don't carry testimonials around with me as proof.'

'Then perhaps I should offer my condolences on your recent set-back in that area!'

As soon as the words were out of her mouth, Kerry regretted them. Where was her normal self-control? Not only was she presenting herself in a bad light by such personal taunting and prejudicing her cause, but she had stooped to an uncalled-for rudeness in referring to unsubstantiated gossip.

'Ah. . .'

His voice had deepened the timbre low and intense so that she was compelled against her will to raise her eyes. It was a mistake. For in that instant she read in his face the existence of a sexuality so acute and blatant that she was forced to draw in a sharp intake of breath to quieten the instinctive reaction of her genes as her heartbeat quickened and the hairs on the back of her neck tingled in a mixture of fear and anticipation.

'So Murray's been priming you on details of my private life, has he?' The gentle question did nothing to allay her alarm.

'It wasn't Murray,' she lied quickly. 'I read about it in one of the Sydney papers.'

'You mustn't believe everything you read.' He regarded her steadily without obvious anger at her presumption. 'Quite a lot of things have been written about me in the past, the majority of which were untrue. However. . .' he paused effectively '. . . I do admit to some of the charges levelled against me—notably a degree of chauvinism on some matters. For instance, I don't care much for a man who sends a woman to fight his battles for him, and I resent the implication that I'm unprincipled enough to be won over by the sight of a pair of hazel eyes, a pretty mouth and a head of flaming red hair—or perhaps you're going to make me an even better offer, hmm?'

'The only thing I'm offering you is the opportunity to behave like a man instead of a monster.' Kerry's eyes sparkled with indignation, but she kept her voice under control with an effort, determined not to rise to his bait. 'And, for the record, Nick didn't send me anywhere! Sam Timpson would never have——'

'Acted so harshly?' He finished her sentence for her. 'I'm aware of that fact, but I think you'll find that from now on our operations manager in Sydney will be reviewing his attitude to such infringements. Tell me, Kerry, what exactly are your motives in trying with so much vigour to get Albioni re-instated?'

Kerry shrugged her shoulders, unwilling to reveal the depth of her involvement to an unsympathetic audience. Let Mel McKinley know that she and Nick Albioni had arranged to spend the fourteen days' rest period to which they were entitled when they finished the tour enjoying each other's company on Dunk Island, and he would take an added delight in thwarting her.

'That hardly matters now, does it? Since your decision is final.'

'On the other hand I wouldn't want you to think I was totally inflexible.' He leaned back in his chair as the waiter removed the empty plates from the table. 'Can I tempt you to a dessert?'

'I don't think so.' She refused to respond to his lazy

smile. 'I ought to be getting back to my unit. I've got to make an early start in the morning.'

'Then we'll just have a liqueur and coffee in the Piano Bar before I take you home.' He rose to his feet, politely pulling the table out so that she could wriggle free from the bench-seat she had chosen.

If she'd thought it would have done any good, Kerry would have protested, one half of her mind telling her that she was fighting a losing battle, the other optimistically reminding her that no battle was won until the last shot had been fired. On balance it was better if she left Mel McKinley on good terms rather than bad—if that were possible.

'Nick's an excellent driver.'

She'd refused another drink, but had gratefully accepted a black coffee, relaxing in one of the darkened, secluded alcoves that were a feature of the small bar. Light, romantic music from the grand piano at one side filled the room, lulling her spirits. Even her companion seemed less formidable as he helped himself to a handful of nuts from the brandy glass on the small table which separated them, and nodded encouragingly.

'I don't know if you're aware of it. . .' She hesitated, then plunged on as his face betrayed only polite interest. 'I work for Metline too, as a hostess.'

'I wondered when you were going to mention that fact.' His strong mouth curled at the corners. 'As a matter of fact, Murray told me when he invited me down to Melbourne for his birthday party.'

Difficult to say from his bland expression how he had accepted the news.

She nodded her head briefly, trying to conceal her own displeasure at the curt way he had treated Murray's invitation, but not totally succeeding. 'He was very disappointed that you were unable to make it.'

'I'm afraid I was particularly busy at the time; besides. . .' his eyes glinted with amusement

'. . .according to company records, Murray's birthday is
in April, not August.'

'Then the records must be wrong,' Kerry said blankly.
'He's certainly not senile, and he'd hardly forget his own
birthday!'

'Precisely.'

Kerry could read nothing from his bland expression.
'That doesn't make any kind of sense.'

She gave the suggestion short shrift, regretting that
she had given him the opportunity to divert her argument, and determined to pursue it. 'But the point I'm
trying to make is that I've had every opportunity to see
Nick in action. We worked together on the Southern
Australia run for a couple of months, and I promise you
he was incredibly popular with all the passengers!'

'And the hostess too?' Sardonic eyebrows questioned
her.

'He's a great guy,' she confirmed stonily. 'We made a
good team and the fact is we'd been matched together
for this coming Queensland tour. It'll be the first time
for me in the area, and I was looking forward to his
showing me the ropes. So I was shocked when he phoned
me last night to tell me what had happened.'

'And suggested that Murray might intervene on his
behalf? So you ran to your grandfather asking him to
pull some strings?'

'Yes.' There was no point in denying it. Nick had
professed himself sick to the gills about the turn of
events, especially as it meant cancelling their joint plans
for a holiday.

'So it was Murray who suggested you use your feminine wiles on me?'

'It wasn't like that at all!' She had no wish to question
Murray's motives further than their face value. 'He just
said it was always better to deal personally with someone
rather than over the telephone.'

'A very percipient man, your grandfather.' Mel

regarded her musingly. 'Are you aware that in the terms of our agreement his fifty-per-cent holding in Metline reverts to McKinleys on his death?'

'Yes. He told me that.' Kerry met his appraisal squarely, surprised by the question. 'Why do you ask?'

'No reason.' His gaze narrowed to pin her with their steely regard. 'I hope you weren't too disappointed by the news?'

'I didn't consider it any of my business!' Her face flamed as she recalled too clearly how Murray had bemoaned the fact that he had nothing to leave her. . .nothing for his great-grandchildren to inherit. He had been the one distressed by the facts—not she!

'Too right, Cinderella! It isn't now and it never will be, so the sooner you get used to the idea, the better!' As Kerry looked at him aghast, groping in her mind for some suitable repartee, he continued lazily, his gaze mercilessly intent on her flushed face, 'I suppose he thought you could win me round with a few flirtatious smiles and appeals to my chivalry?'

'What chivalry?' Eyebrows flaring towards her hairline, Kerry mocked him. 'If anything, I hoped to appeal to your business sense. Nick and I have a proven record, and he knows the route well. Now I shall be working with a stranger on an unknown route.'

'And with your resourceful nature I'm sure you'll cope very well. Take comfort in the fact that it's company policy always to ensure that either the driver or the hostess is familiar with the route, so you can be assured the guy with you will be experienced.'

'I see Murray was right when he called you "intract-able".' With as much dignity as she could muster Kerry drained her coffee-cup, rising to her feet. 'Thank you for the meal, it was very enjoyable.' She managed to convey that the food had been delicious but the company far less satisfactory. 'I can find my own way home.'

She didn't wait for his response, edging her slim body

between the tables, intent on escaping without a further trade of contentious words. She supposed if she annoyed him sufficiently he wouldn't be past dispensing with her services too—and on a long-term basis! Not that she'd be worried, but it would be humiliating to have to face Murray with such a summary dismissal.

Already she felt a little guilty about quoting him out of context. On the occasion her grandfather had called Mel McKinley 'intractable' he had used it in the sense of being steadfast rather than cantankerous, as she had deliberately implied.

Walking quickly, she found her way easily to the foyer, smiling her thanks to the doorman as the door was promptly opened for her. On the steps she hesitated for a bare second, trying to get her bearings in the warm darkness, when she felt her arm firmly taken.

'You're not safe to be allowed out by yourself with all that temper seething away inside you.'

Calmly, and with adamantine purpose, Mel McKinley ushered her into a waiting taxi. 'I said I'd see you home, and that's precisely what I mean to do.' He held up a peremptory hand as she started to protest. 'Be a good girl, Kerry, and give the driver your address, or we'll have to spend the rest of the evening cruising round the town.'

He meant it. Besides, no one in her right mind would prefer to travel by underground as opposed to taxi— although she would have preferred a choice of companion. Leaning forward, she gave her address to the driver as instructed.

Robbed of the satisfaction of snubbing any attempt at conversation because her infuriating escort made no effort to converse, Kerry contented herself with staring out of the window as the taxi left the lights of the city behind on its way to the suburbs.

CHAPTER THREE

TWENTY minutes later Kerry was at her destination.

'I'll wish you goodnight, then.' She flashed her escort an insincere smile.

Having hoped that he would merely redirect the taxi back to his hotel, her heart sank as he followed her out on to the pavement with a curt request to the driver to wait.

'I'll see you right to your front door.' Lightly he touched her elbow, and guided her through the pleasant garden. If she'd been alone she would have paused to savour the sweetly scented air, the stillness of the winter night and the brilliance of the stars. With Mel McKinley in such close proximity, her only thought was to get the front door firmly closed between them.

Fumbling for her key in her bag, irritatingly aware that he was patiently waiting for her to find it, she muttered under her breath.

'Give it to me.' He took it from her shaking fingers as soon as they had closed on it, turning it easily in her lock and pushing the door gently inwards before removing the key and placing it once more in her palm. His hand was warm and capable, closing with a gentle pressure on her nervous fingers as she murmured unwilling thanks.

'Not at all; my pleasure.' The words were trite, and if she'd moved away at that moment she could have been safely inside without further incident. But something kept her rooted to the spot as the softly moving shadows of graceful trees turned the strong masculine face so very close to her own into a strange territory. Grey eyes were suddenly softer, their smile genuine rather than sarcastic; the beautifully contoured mouth became a fount of soft promises as Kerry's pulse responded to the strange magic by thrumming like a feeding humming-bird's wings.

When Mel McKinley took both her shoulders in his hands and gazed down into her upraised face she read the intention in those compelling eyes and found herself frozen to immobility. His mouth was warm and soft as it caressed her parted lips. Mentally she rejected him, but somehow the message didn't reach her mouth. It was no more than a gentle brush of sensitive skin, leaving her with a tingling sensation of frustration as he stepped away from her, and she could have wept with disappointment at her own vulnerability.

'I'm sorry you've had such an unsuccessful evening.' His patronising tone compounded her vexation. 'But you know what they say—you can't win them all.'

'You should know!' she responded tartly, tilting her chin defiantly at him. Furious because he had dared to caress her mouth with such fleeting, condescending liberty, she forsook the caution which would normally have restrained the urge to bait him.

'Oh, I have my share of frustration too,' he acknowledged smoothly. 'But I try to make sure it doesn't interfere with my work, so make sure you're on time tomorrow.' Was it her imagination or did his voice sound deeper, curdled with some emotion she couldn't name? 'There's no room for slackers or hangers-on in my organisation.'

Kerry didn't wait to see him go, gaining the sanctuary of her small hall without delay, and sinking down in the nearest chair as her legs turned to aspic. It had been an abortive mission, and she would have fared better staying at home and reading a good book! She supposed she'd better pull herself together and phone Nick with the bad news before going to bed.

'I suppose you did your best,' he said sulkily, after listening to her detailing of events. 'I guess I expected too much from you.'

'I guess you did at that!' It had hardly been her fault if Mel McKinley was a hard-hearted tyrant who seemed to take pleasure in thwarting lesser mortals, and she was just as disappointed as Nick was, wasn't she? Yet from his attitude anyone would think *she* was to blame for the demolition of their plans! And a little commiseration at the ordeal she'd suffered would have been welcome! She replaced the phone unable to quell the sense of disillusionment she was feeling at Nick's total disregard of her own misery at the way things had turned out.

Instead of counting sheep she'd go through the alphabet finding an adjective which would adequately describe the man who had just left her doorstep. Starting with 'arrogant' and ending with 'zealous', she had no doubt but that she would find a list that would go some way to putting her feelings into words! She reached 'overbearing' before becoming overtaken by sleep.

The following morning she was up early, taking her usual pleasure in dressing herself in the smart Metline uniform. Congratulating Murray on an outfit she would have accepted quite happily into her personal wardrobe, she'd been surprised when he'd given credit for it to the new director.

'Mel asked one of the new young Australian designers to create something a little different,' he'd told her. 'He felt that to look good would add to the hostesses' pleasure in the job, which would in its turn benefit the customers.'

Resent him as she did, Kerry could see the good sense behind the assumption, and grudgingly admitted that his decision had been a wise one. Not only had the uniform of his choice been smart, with its soft pleated skirt and well-tailored bolero over a beautifully cut blouse, but, even more important, it was easy to wear, enabling the girls to do the hundred and one jobs for which they were responsible comfortably and with dignity.

Once they crossed the Tropic of Capricorn to enter the Torrid Zone, and the heat intensified, she would change into the cotton dress which was a longer version of the blouse and which, too, had been designed to provide coolness with ease of movement.

Her eyes sparkling with excitement, she determined to put the disappointment of the previous day behind her. For one thing her training had taught her to be a professional, which meant keeping calm, pleasant and helpful at all times. For another, she was really looking forward to sampling a new route and learning more about the country where her father had been born. With Nick it would have been perfect, but all Metline's drivers were chosen with great care, and there was no reason to suppose she would be incompatible with the substitute who would take his place.

Brushing her wealth of red-gold hair, taming its tangles, she confined it in a neat bunch at the nape of her neck, tied it with a navy ribbon, and surveyed her reflection critically. An unremarkable face, she decided with a grin at her own vanity. How pleasant it would have been to have had the classic features of a Nordic ice-maiden, or the sultry beauty of a Latin flamenco dancer. Perhaps in those circumstances her mission with Mel McKinley would have been successful! He wasn't a man who would be impervious to feminine beauty, she mused, remembering the latent fires she had glimpsed behind his cool appraisal. On the other hand it would have been demeaning to have used physical beauty as a weapon, so perhaps it was just as well she looked like the typical 'girl next door', even to the sprinkling of freckles which scattered across her high cheekbones.

Two cups of freshly brewed coffee and a bowl of cereal with the last of the milk in the fridge and she was ready—well ahead of time. With a last look around to ensure everything was in order, she picked up her small suitcase and left the unit, breathing in the fresh morning air with a deep sigh of contentment as she made her way to the nearest underground entrance.

The Metline waiting-room was also new. A one-storey glass and steel building comprising a comfortable lounge for passengers who arrived early and an office in which the hostesses and drivers picked up their final briefs which would supply them with the names, addresses and nationalities of their passengers, together with a seating plan.

There were already a few passengers waiting when she entered, and she gave them a friendly smile as she passed through to the office.

'Kerry Davies,' she introduced herself to the young man behind the desk. 'I'm taking the Cairns Tour.'

'Hello, Kerry.' He gave her a brief, warm smile, holding out a folder towards her. 'Here's your passenger manifesto. Haven't seen you here before. I take it you're new on this run?'

'Uh-huh.' She took the folder. 'Pretty new to the company, too,' she added ruefully. 'Can you tell me who my driver is?'

'Nope!' He grinned at her worried face. 'Was going to be Nick Albioni, but I gather he's—uh—indisposed. But don't worry, they'll find a relief man. You won't be expected to drive the coach as well as chat up the passengers!'

Kerry smiled weakly at his attempt at humour, wishing she didn't have so many butterflies fluttering about in her tummy. There was no need to panic, she told herself firmly, or to suppose she wouldn't get on with the driver. After all, they were all chosen for their social graces as well as their ability to handle a coach, plus their knowledge of the terrain and an ability to comment on the countryside with ease and exactitude as they passed through it. It was just that she would feel a lot better when she'd come face to face with the man under whose direction she'd be working for the next fourteen days.

'Look, why don't you take a seat and study the

manifesto?' the desk clerk suggested kindly. 'You won't be needed until all the passengers have been seated by the terminus receptionists, and you'll get a good idea of what you're going to have to deal with in advance. I'll give you a shout when your driver puts in an appearance.'

'Thanks.' Kerry accepted the suggestion gracefully, seating herself on a functional straight-back chair, her suitcase at her feet, and giving her attention to the list in her hands.

'You certainly do seem to make a virtue of arriving on the scene early, sweetheart.'

'Oh!' Shocked at hearing a voice she would know anywhere spoken so close to her ear. Kerry riveted upright-turning, reproachful eyes on the amused countenance of Mel McKinley, who had approached her so quietly that she'd been totally unaware of his presence. 'What are you doing here?'

Mocking grey eyes took their toll of her beneath dark, cleanly shaped, level brows. 'Just checking that the wheels are running smoothly, what else? Why? Do you object to my presence?'

For some unaccountable reason, she did. She was tense enough, having to face a new route and an unknown driver plus forty or more strangers who were relying on her to see their holiday went without a hitch, without having to put up with Mel McKinley's contentious proximity as well. Already her heart had increased its beat as adrenalin rushed to her aid, bringing a slight flush to her cheeks and a sparkle to her eyes as well as increasing the effect of the Lepidoptera banging themselves against her ribs.

'I object to your insinuation that punctuality is some kind of sin,' she returned smartly. 'And I also object to your calling me "sweetheart",' she added primly for good measure.

'That's because of your prissy English upbringing, I

guess,' he told her easily. Was she imagining it, or was he deliberately emphasising the slight drawl which characterised his speech?

'It's because I happen to think that using terms of endearment without meaning cheapens them—and the person to whom they're applied!'

'My, you really do carry a grudge, don't you?' He didn't seem disconcerted, though, as he allowed his gaze to dwell on her face for several seconds before dropping it to survey the rest of her tautly held body. 'What's this?'

She followed the direction of his eyes, holding her breath, feeling the tension between them begin to quiver, but determined not to offer more than she was required to give. 'My suitcase.'

'Not to take with you today, sweetheart, it isn't.' Steel-grey eyes dared her to challenge his decree. 'Don't you know luggage capacity is one of our big problems because we're limited by safety precautions?'

'Yes, of course I know that. . .' she began a little desperately, inwardly cursing the malignant fate which had decreed his presence on this particular day, and wishing she'd been a little less tart with him in her own interests. Now he was prepared to offer her no quarter. She knew that, not only from the sudden coldness of his expression, but from the way he had deliberately used the word 'sweetheart', loading it with the scorn of an insult.

'But naturally, because of your *special* relationship with Albioni, you considered yourself an exception to the rule that staff carry a minimum of luggage? Or was it because you thought that being Murray's granddaughter made you more privileged than the rest of your colleagues?'

'Neither of those things!' Kerry cried heatedly, scrambling to her feet, tired of having him towering over her. Not that standing up improved the position greatly. He was still several inches taller than she, not to mention broader. . .

'I know it's not normal practice and, believe me, it's the first time I've ever done it, but when we reach Cairns I'm due for two weeks' holiday, so I was hoping that there'd be spare capacity in the luggage compartment for it.'

There was nothing to be read from his impassive face as she struggled on. 'I couldn't see myself spending two weeks on Dunk Island with nothing to wear but my uniform!'

'So you hope to persuade the driver to break the rules and load it on for you?'

'Only if it doesn't break state legislation.'

'In that case, you'd better start repacking.'

Kerry swallowed miserably, unable to make up her mind whether his terse instruction was justified or whether he was just being provocative—demonstrating the power he wielded within the company. For the sake of her future comfort she would have to make one more appeal—even though past experience told her it would be futile.

'Surely it should be the driver's decision when he arrives?' she asked, wondering if any driver would dare to lock horns with Mel McKinley.

'Oh, Kerry. . .' The gleam in those gimlet eyes promised her nothing but trouble. 'And here was I thinking what a bright girl you are. Do you mean to say that you still haven't realised that your driver has already arrived?'

'He has?' She'd been so engrossed that she hadn't paid any attention recently to the comings and goings in the office. Now, as she half turned to gain a clear view, she saw a middle-aged man wearing the Metline uniform in deep conversation with the desk clerk. 'Then let's ask him. . .' She made a quick movement in the man's direction only to find herself halted by a firm hand on her arm.

'Not Jack Ferguson, Kerry. He's taking the Winter Capital tour to Adelaide. It's *me* you have to deal with. *I've* decided to take Nick Albioni's place.'

'You're joking!' Even as the words burst from her lips, Kerry's sinking heart told her he wasn't. For the first time she realised that he was wearing the dark navy trousers and pale blue short-sleeved shirt that was the Metline uniform for its male members. On Mel McKinley it hadn't looked like a uniform at all. His physique had somehow dominated it, transforming it into a fashion accessory to his own persona. Even as he shook his head, she grasped at the final straw. 'You're not wearing a tie!'

'Sorry.' He didn't look in the least remorseful as he reached inside his trouser-pocket and produced the necessary item, proceeding to put it into place under her disconcerted gaze.

'But you can't. . .you're a director, not a driver. . . Every driver has to know the route if the hostess doesn't. . .' The garbled phrases poured from her angry lips.

'Because I *am* a director I can do what I please,' he told her civilly enough. 'And at the moment it pleases me to go out on the road. If it's my driving ability which worries you, I can assure you I have every necessary qualification, and as for knowing the route, well, when I first joined the company my father made sure that I drove over every route over which we operated. It's a practice I still follow—even though he's no longer with us. Rest assured I know what I'm doing and where I'm going!'

As if she had ever doubted it!

'I—I'm not sure I want to be your hostess.' She faced Mel squarely, unable to quantify the emotions which bubbled inside her. 'I mean, it's vital the driver and the hostess should get on together for the sake of the passengers. . .'

'I'm delighted you realise that.' His imperturbable
gaze lingered on her face. 'But surely that's just a matter
of professionalism? Or perhaps you're uncertain of your
own performance?' He challenged her, keeping his voice
level and unemotional. 'I can't stop you resigning here
and now if that's the case. There's no problem in
replacing you—although it will mean keeping the passengers waiting, and I dare say Murray will be disappointed, but if that's the way it is. . .'

Kerry had only seconds to make up her mind. All the
things he'd said were valid, and she had no wish to
disappoint her grandfather or delay the passengers, and
why should she let Mel McKinley rob her of her eagerly
anticipated holiday—even if it did mean she would have
to spend some of her savings on more clothes when she
reached her destination?

'You're right!' she said briskly, reaching her decision
with alacrity. 'As you say, it's simply a matter of
professionalism.' She stooped to grab her suitcase. 'It
will only take me a few minutes to get this repacked.'

'Wait!' A strong hand seized her wrist and continued
to hold it so that she was unable to retreat. 'You had no
intention of staying on Dunk alone, did you? Nick
Albioni was going with you.'

'That's my affair, not yours!' she retorted hotly, aware
too late of her unhappy choice of words.

'Wrong, sweetheart!' He pounced on her prevari-
cation. 'We don't encourage romances between our
couriers, even the single ones without commitments, but
one thing we won't tolerate is adultery. In case you
haven't noticed, the majority of our passengers are of the
age group who were born before the permissive society
was. They still have moral standards.'

Kerry flinched, her throat tightening with shock.
Nick, married? It was impossible. He'd never mentioned
a wife. 'Nick's not married!'

Mel was deliberately baiting her for his own amusement, and she wasn't going to fall into his trap by
pouring out her assurances that she and Nick had never
done anything which would offend the strictest puritan
on the board. From the numbed recesses of her mind
came the evidence which would prove Mel McKinley's
calumny. 'He lives with his mother!'

'Sure he does.' His tone was hard and goading.
'Because his wife has taken his two other children back
to Italy to await the birth of the third little Albioni.
Seems she likes to be with her own mother at such
momentous times.'

Children too! There had to be some mistake! Surely
Nick wasn't the kind of man to deny the existence of a
family? Mel's nearness was unbalancing, making it difficult for her to defend herself as she tried to escape the
brutal tightness of his fingers, her gaze flicking over his
tanned, chiselled face with its accusing grey eyes.

Obligingly he released her, more, she supposed bitterly, to avoid their becoming the centre of attention
rather than in deference to her discomfort.

'You have no proof!' she accused wildly, fighting a
growing conviction that he might be right, and already
grateful that she hadn't got as far as commiting herself
either physically or emotionally to the handsome
Italianate driver.

He regarded her with cool detachment. 'Sorry, sweetheart. It's all down on the company records.'

'The same records which have fouled up Murray's
birthday!'

Mel treated her outburst with the silent contempt it
deserved. A computer operator might have programmed
'Aug' instead of 'Apr', but no one was inefficient enough
to give a single man a wife and three children. Three
children! Uncertainly Kerry swept her troubled eyes
over Mel's commanding face. He stared back at her, cool
and collected, his expression sardonic.

'But—but. . .' she stammered unhappily, finally accepting what logic told her must be true. 'I had no idea. He never mentioned any wife or children, and Italians are supposed to be so fond of their families, aren't they?'

'This one was obviously fonder of continuing his love-life outside marriage.'

'I had no idea. . .' she repeated distractedly. 'Not that it would have made any difference to our friendship, because. . .'

'That's what I expected you to say.' Mel's disdainful gaze scanned her taut face. 'Well, who am I to preach? My own philosophy is based on an old Spanish proverb which loosely translated says "Take what you want—and pay for it!" The problem is deciding just how high a price one is prepared to pay!'

'Mel, you don't understand. . .' Appalled that he had put his own incorrect interpretation on the sentence he had interrupted, Kerry laid a placatory hand on his arm, anxious now to explain that, to date, her relationship with Nick Albioni had been purely platonic with the emphasis on the 'pure', and to emphasise that she would never have agreed to have gone on holiday with him in any circumstances if she'd known he was married. But before she could collect her thoughts he stooped to pick up her suitcase.

'You do me an injustice, Kerry,' he told her drily. 'I understand very well how easy it is to be deceived by a beautiful profile, but we can't argue about it now. Come along, there's no time for repacking. I'm sure we'll find a space for the contents of your wardrobe somewhere.'

'Thank you.' The words were uttered stiffly, and earned her a sharp, appraising glance as she followed Mel to the door, still trying to come to terms with what she had learned about a man she had trusted.

'You're welcome. You'll find swimming's no problem on Dunk because there's a nudist beach, but you'd look rather bizarre horse-riding in your birthday suit and a crash helmet, and the Metline uniform wasn't designed for such rigorous exercise!'

He paused, and for one awful moment Kerry imagined he was visualising her either sunbathing or riding in the way he had speculated as his glance passed swiftly over her. Then the glimmer of laughter which had aroused her suspicions died from his eyes.

'You may have got your own way on this occasion, sweetheart, but don't count on it again, will you? There are nearly two thousand miles and fourteen days before we reach Cairns, and I intend to watch you every waking hour of the day and every mile of the way. Put one foot wrong, break one company rule, be the cause of one passenger complaining, and even the fact of Murray Davies being your grandfather won't save your hide!'

CHAPTER FOUR

KERRY switched off her blow-dryer and surveyed her gleaming strands of red-gold hair. Over the past two weeks she'd taken to using a coconut-oil shampoo in order to tame its exuberance and condition it against the power of the tropical sun, and the results were definitely gratifying.

Laying down the dryer, she walked to her bed, lifting the neat blue and white striped dress of her uniform to draw it on over her shoulders, fastening the bodice buttons, neatening the neckline, and tying the material belt loosely round her slender waist, happily aware that it was the last time she would be doing so for the next fortnight.

Somehow she had managed to survive nearly two thousand miles and fourteen days without drawing down Mel McKinley's wrath on her defenceless head. She'd worked hard—if taking part in such a glorious sightseeing tour of the Queensland coast could be called working—spreading her attention equally among those who desired it, being careful not to attract Mel's censure by appearing to give more of her time to a favoured few. She smiled to herself. At one time it had looked as if a young Englishman travelling alone had definite designs to appropriate her services to an unfair degree, but fortunately she'd managed to dissuade him without giving offence, and had taken smug satisfaction in seeing Colin pursuing in her stead a Dutch teenager on holiday with her parents.

Her role was to act as a personal assistant to all the passengers, helping with anything from banking and hairdressing information to such essentials as the speediest way to get laundry processed at their nightly stops, and where to post mail, as well as organising and preparing lunchtime barbecues for everybody on the occasions when their midday stop was miles away from any township; and she thought she had coped efficiently with all the duties which had been thrust upon her.

It hadn't been easy, with the awareness of Mel's eagle-like eyes scrutinising her every action, but her three months' training at Metline's special school in Melbourne had been as rigorous as that for any air hostess, covering courses on bush survival, first aid and driving, as well as tact and courtesy. She'd been thrilled to graduate from the course at her first attempt and with high marks!

Conscious that part of Mel's antipathy towards her sprung from his misbegotten belief that Murray had somehow pulled strings on her behalf, she had been grimly determined to prove her worth. She thought she had succeeded, but was in no doubt that he would make his opinion known to her in due course before they parted tomorrow.

Returning to the mirror, she applied a light dusting of powder to her face before defining her eyebrows and darkening her long lashes with a waterproof mascara, then stood back, frowning slightly at her reflection. Not the kind of girl at all whose looks would lure a married man away from his wife and children, surely?

She sighed, dismissing Nick's mendacity from her thoughts. Time enough to deal with that when she saw him again! She'd make quite sure he knew the kind of ordeal she had been called upon to face because of his moral irresponsibility! Not that she cared one whit for Mel McKinley's disdain, only that she hadn't merited it, and injustice always rankled!

On the table beside her bed the telephone sprang into sudden life.

'Hello, Kerry, love. So what do you think of the "Sunshine State"?'

'Murray!' Delighted to hear the familiar voice, she plumped down on the bed. 'I think it's absolutely fabulous. I don't know how I'm ever going to tear myself away from this marvellous country.'

'Then don't!' His deep voice sounded extra-gruff over the wire. 'Nothing would please me better than for you to make your future home here.'

'I'll think about it,' she promised lightly. 'Did you get my postcards? I sent one at every stop we made.'

'Couldn't wait for the postman to deliver each morning!' His chuckle sounded clearly in her ear. 'Seems like you got more than you bargained for when you took up cudgels for your young Italian friend. How are you getting on with the notorious Mel McKinley?'

'Huh! Notorious is just about the right word!' Perhaps the telephone wasn't the ideal instrument over which to vent her feelings, but they'd been bottled up so long that the promise of a sympathetic ear was too much. 'Honestly, Murray—the man's impossible. He's prejudiced, a slave-driver, rude, unfeeling. . .a right pain in the——'

'Whoa, whoa!' Murray was actually laughing at her vehemence. 'You're talking about our beloved chairman and managing director, as well as a personal friend of mine.'

'Well, he's certainly no friend of mine,' she told him tartly, 'and as for being beloved, don't forget it was you who told me that even his girlfriend had seen through the surface charm to the dross beneath it!'

'Tt, tt. . . I think I'm being misquoted. If anyone was dross beneath the gold then it was Belinda Fraser, not Mel. Sounds like he's been giving you a hard time, though—what have you been up to?'

'Me?' Kerry's voice rose to a squeak of indignation. 'I can assure you I've been a model of industry and affability despite all the trials that have been visited on me. Your dear friend Mel appears to be under the impression that I was given this job out of the kindness of your heart rather than on just deserts!'

Now was not the time to elucidate on the part Nick had played in creating the vibrant atmosphere which existed between them! In fact, she doubted she would ever tell Murray how Nick had misled her. Her grandfather was the kind of man who would take up the cudgels on her behalf and, although she appreciated the support she knew she would get from him, the idea of becoming the centre of a company scandal was not appealing!

'Fair enough.' Murray didn't sound in the least disturbed by the accusation. 'I'm sure you've proved how wrong he is.'

'Hopefully!' Kerry gritted her teeth, refraining by an almighty effort from telling her grandfather of Mel's threat. Presumably his warning as to the vulnerability of her hide was metaphorical rather than literal, though in view of the gleam in his grey eyes as he'd uttered the warning she wouldn't be prepared to take a bet on it!

Again Murray's laughter echoed down the line. 'I like his style, Kerry. In many ways, you know, he reminds me of Warren. The same stubborn determination, a sense of purpose and ambition, and a fierce loyalty.'

'But however did my mother cope?' Horror deepened her voice. 'I mean, Louise is such a gentle, helpless person. . .'

For a moment she thought the silence at the other end of the line meant they'd been cut off, then she heard Murray sigh.

'They were happy enough for the brief time they had together. Who knows how the marriage would have matured? Louise was a dear girl, but I always thought Warren needed a woman with a spirit to match his own—in the same way *you* need a man like McKinley to match your flame and burn brighter with it.'

This time it was Kerry who laughed, a peal of uncontrolled amusement. 'Darling Murray! You're way off beam! We detest each other!'

'Pity,' he retorted mildly. 'Because the only way I can ensure my bloodline continues in the business I started is for McKinley to father my great-grandchildren.'

'Murray!' Her horror at his remark was only superseded by a terrible suspicion. 'How long have you been thinking along those lines?'

'Since I first saw what a beautiful granddaughter Warren had given me,' he told her without shame. 'I had this gut feeling that if the two of you ever met there'd be fireworks.'

Fireworks weren't in it—an explosion in a munitions factory more likely, she thought desperately, and if she wasn't wildly mistaken Murray had gone to some lengths to try and engineer just such a meeting!

'Murray,' she demanded sternly. 'Did you ever mention this vision of dynasty to McKinley?'

'I might have done.' He sounded quite impatient. 'I seem to remember telling him that you were worth ten Belinda Frasers. Poor guy was like a wallaby with a thorn in its foot—hopping mad—when he arrived on the east coast from Perth,' he continued, presumably trying to justify his actions. 'Thought I'd point out that there were other, tastier fish in the sea.'

Kerry's suspicions hardened.

'When exactly is your birthday?' she asked peremptorily, her tone daring him to lie to her.

His hesitation told her all she needed to know. Oh, dear heavens! He had contrived a rendezvous, and Mel had seen right through his subterfuge. No wonder he had turned down the invitation to the mythical birthday celebration. She went hot then cold at the thought of it. Then Murray had manipulated her into approaching his partner on a mission he must have known would be a failure from the start. It had been a blatant example of attempted matchmaking which hadn't fooled Mel McKinley for one moment. Thank the powers-that-be that after tonight she need never set eyes on him again!

Holding back her indignation at what he had done, Kerry said goodbye to Murray, knowing even in her turmoil that he had thought he was acting in her interests as well as his own. Forcing herself to assume a composure she was far from feeling, she went down to join the passengers for the farewell party.

In the veranda restaurant the celebrations were drawing to their close, addresses being exchanged, the pleasure of the final dinner being dimmed by the knowledge that this was the last time that they, the passengers, would exist as a separate entity, cocooned in their luxury coach, cosseted and pampered over nearly two thousand miles.

Tonight had been especially gratifying too, as it was the golden wedding anniversary of a couple from Adelaide. One of her duties having been to ascertain such causes for celebration, Kerry had asked the hotel to provide a special cake as a surprise. Since Mel had added to the festivities by ordering a top-class Australian champagne to be served with it, the party had really swung. Warmed by the knowledge that the tour had been totally successful, Kerry sipped her wine with the appreciation of a connoisseur.

'Can I have your attention for a moment?'

It was the Australian who had been celebrating his golden wedding, raising his voice to command silence.

'I've been asked to speak on behalf of all of us to thank Mel and Kerry for their help and the pleasure of their company over the past two weeks.'

Cries of 'Hear, hear' greeted his words, as smiling faces beamed on the two of them.

'Since deeds speak louder than words, we've had a bit

of a whip-round, and we'd like to ask Mel to accept this small token of our appreciation on behalf of both of them!'

As a round of applause broke out, Mel rose lazily to his feet.

'Kerry. . .' An autocratic arm lifted to summon her to his side. Reluctantly she joined him in the centre of the floor. 'I'm sure I speak for both of us when I say we've enjoyed having you aboard, and look forward to seeing you all again next year. On behalf of my hostess and myself, I thank you all for being such perfect passengers, and for your very generous gesture. We are both very touched and delighted with your gift.'

He accepted a small box with a slot in the lid, as Kerry, murmuring her own thanks, managed to escape from the strong arm he'd thrown about her shoulders, disturbed by the friendly proximity of his strong male body.

Outside in the hotel garden the full moon was reflected in the motionless waters of the swimming-pool. Grateful for the silence of the warm night, Kerry walked slowly beneath the massive mango trees. Earlier that evening they had been alive with brilliant-feathered, chattering lorikeets, now they were empty and still. Her gaze drifted upwards, her bright eyes searching for the constellation known as the Southern Cross, as a sense of peace enveloped her.

'Kerry?'

A tall figure had emerged from the shadows, making her pulse leap and the adrenalin flow as she supposed she had identified Mel. An odd feeling—not disappointment, surely?—followed the moment he moved closer to her, and she saw it was the young Englishman who had turned his attentions to Marijka van Houten when she had made it clear she wasn't interested in forming a more personal relationship with him.

'Hello, Colin.' She smiled her professional smile. 'What can I do for you?'

'Give me a goodbye kiss to remember you by.' He stood in front of her, barring her progress. 'That's not too much to ask, is it?'

'So you can brag to the guys back home that you had something going with the hostess?' she retorted, smiling. 'What about Marijka? How many strings to your bow do you want?'

'I only ever wanted one—you!' He moved closer to her so she could smell the alcohol on his breath and discern from his muted belligerence that he had imbibed slightly more of the champagne than he could carry. 'Only your boyfriend gave me the hands-off message in capitals! But seeing as how he's not around at the moment, and I won't be seeing you again after tomorrow morning, how about a kiss to show there's no hard feeling?'

Boyfriend indeed! She didn't need to ask Colin to whom he was referring. Mel McKinley's heavy-handedness where she was concerned was shining like a beacon. Presumably he didn't trust her capabilities of looking after herself—or perhaps he actually thought she would welcome a liaison with a passenger, in view of what he considered her previous history to be, although this was strictly forbidden by company rules?

It was while these thoughts were tumbling through her mind that Colin pounced. Taking her momentary silence for tacit agreement, he grabbed her shoulders, drawing her close, pressing his hungry mouth over her own with a force which prevented any cry of protest she might have made. For several seconds there was nothing she could do but endure the passion of his kiss, finding solace in the fact that at least his hands, firmly pressed against her back, were showing no signs of taking further liberties with her unresponsive body.

'I guess I owe you an apology.' He had the grace to

look ashamed as he released her. 'It's just that I thought, well you know how it is. . . Sometimes a kiss can get things rolling even if the initial response isn't very encouraging.'

'That sounds a very dangerous philosophy to me.' Kerry kept her voice coolly detached although her heart was thumping with indignation. 'I hope that after tonight you'll reconsider before using it.'

He was still mumbling apologies as she walked briskly away and disappeared into the well-lit foyer of the hotel.

She touched her mouth a trifle ruefully. Colin needed to learn a lot. Obviously he was one of those men who confused passion with force, and the sheer blind chauvinism of a man who believed that his kisses had the power to turn 'no' into 'yes'. Far from feeling any *frissons* of desire, all she'd experienced in his hold was a burning desire to escape!

Marching angrily along the long corridor towards the bend beyond which lay her single room, she was glad she had managed to deal with Colin firmly without giving undue offence.

'Oh!' The exclamation burst from her slightly swollen lips as she turned the corner into the small corridor at the end of which her room was situated, to find Mel McKinley, leaning against her door, legs crossed, arms akimbo.

'Ah. At last.' He made no effort to move. 'I was wondering how long it would take you to tear yourself out of lover-boy's arms.' He glanced down at his watch. 'Much sooner than I expected, I admit—but perhaps he's joining you here?'

'No, he's not!'

Damn, damn, damn! Trust him to have been lurking around in the shadows when Colin had had his aberration. But she was darned if she was going to explain what had happened. It wasn't as if he would believe her, anyway, and nothing was going to make her do anything that would make Mel McKinley think she valued his opinion of her.

'Ah. . .then perhaps you're a lady who prefers to visit the gentleman?' he drawled, a look of spurious interest raising his level brows.

'Even if that were the case,' Kerry said between her teeth, 'I'd be right out of luck on this tour, wouldn't I? Not a gentleman in sight! And now, if you'd stop doing your impression of a eunuch outside a harem door, I'd like to get into my room.'

'What a challenging choice of words,' he commented softly, and for a moment she thought nothing was going to shift the solid mass of his lean body. Then he moved lazily, indicating she put her key in the lock.

Trembling with pent-up fury, Kerry did as she was bade, fumbling a little before it turned. To her dismay he was right behind her as she stepped across the threshold.

'Will you please get out of my room,' she stated curtly, turning to face him, her face set, her chin high. 'It may have escaped your notice, but it's past midnight and the tour has officially ended. I'm free to do what I like, with whom I like, without breaking company regulations. As far as I'm concerned I'm on holiday now and you have no jurisdiction over me whatsoever.'

'Very few things escape my notice, Kerry.' Mel's gaze fastened on her abused lips. It was impossible to stop the blood flushing her cheeks as Kerry saw the knowing tilt of his own mouth. 'Plays a little rough, doesn't he? But perhaps you prefer it that way?'

'Did you want anything particular, or have you just come here to be obnoxious?' She regarded him stonily.

'Both,' he told her promptly. 'If being obnoxious means questioning your choice of boyfriends. I dare say there's not a lot wrong with Colin that a few more years' experience and a couple of hard lessons from life won't put right, but in the meantime he's no match for you, sweetheart. You need a lot more than moonlight and mangoes, Kerry, to give you sweet dreams.'

'The one thing I don't need is your interference in my affairs. I'm quite capable of handling the passengers by myself.' She kept her temper with an effort, determined not to give him the satisfaction of seeing how much his impertinent comments had incensed her, and, purposefully ignoring his *sotto voce* 'That's what I was afraid of sweetheart', she added, 'If that's the obnoxious bit over, could we deal with the particular purpose of your visit?'

'Certainly.' He thrust his hands into the back pocket of his close-fitting trousers and produced a roll of banknotes. 'I had the collection taken on our behalf changed up into larger notes. These are for you.'

'But there's nearly two hundred dollars here!'

Mel nodded. 'Shows we did a good job, eh? Come in handy for your holiday, too.'

'But this was meant to be shared between us!' Even then it was a generous contribution when the company stated that gratuities were included in the cost of the tour, and anything over and above was entirely at the discretion of the passengers.

'Possibly,' Mel shrugged. 'But in the first place they weren't aware that I wasn't earning my living driving a coach, and in the second, I'm sure most of it was a tribute to *your* charm and personality.'

'But——' she began to protest.

'Oh, dear,' he sighed with mock anguish. 'You're not going to be difficult about this, are you?'

'I don't want to take money from you which I haven't earned,' she said stubbornly, her eyes flashing fire into the steely depths of his languid stare, wishing with all her heart that he'd go away and leave her to prepare for the early-morning departure.

'And how would you like to earn it, I wonder?' He regarded her musingly as her eyes widened in shocked recognition of the underlying current of meaning in his deep voice.

'I don't know what I've done to deserve this!' Kerry's heart thundered in her breast at his audacity. 'But you can take the money—all the money—and get lost! I don't have to take orders from you now.'

'But a little advice might do you some good.' He ignored her outstretched hand as she waved it imperatively at him, inviting him to repossess the bundle of notes.

Frustrated by his cool disdain, Kerry made an elementary error, attempting to thrust the dollars into the breast-pocket of his casual shirt. Instantly her hand was seized and held in position against the warmth of his chest.

'Stop playing games, Kerry,' he told her. 'Unless you're prepared to lose. Almost from the first moment we met you've been challenging my masculinity, inviting me to prove myself as a red-blooded male. . .'

'No!' She denied it vigorously, her eyes widening in absolute horror. The most she could be accused of was indulging in a little repartee now and again to avoid appearing to be a sycophant.

'Oh, but yes!' Mel smiled down at her upturned face. 'Little digs here and there because you were smart enough to realise I wouldn't seek retribution while we were working as a team. Someone ought to explain to you that it's very unwise to suggest to a man that he's a eunuch. It creates a situation crying out for elucidation.'

'Let me go!' she hissed, cursing herself silently that the attempt to get her own back on him had rebounded so drastically against her. 'You know that was a joke!'

'Do I?' His smile deepened.

Eyes mesmerised by the disarming cleft in his chin, Kerry wondered why it was that her fury at the situation in which she'd found herself was not augmented by fear. Somewhere deep inside herself she knew Mel McKinley wouldn't harm her—ruffle her feathers a little, dent her pride a mite, but never inflict a real injury on her. Despite her certainty her blood continued to race through her veins and her pulse to hammer as if she'd just completed a two-hour marathon.

'And was making a public exhibition of yourself with the amorous Colin a joke too?' His free hand rose to caress one of her flushed cheeks. 'Something to bring a smile to my face because you knew I was only a few yards behind you and would get a stalls view of the performance?'

For a moment Kerry was unable to find the words she needed to refute such a bizarre suggestion. Too conscious of the agitated rise and fall of her breasts beneath the thin cotton of her dress, and the way her legs seemed to be turning to rubber, she could only make inarticulate noises in her throat.

'Precisely,' he murmured, just as if she had made some startling confession. 'And, believe me, from where I was standing it was a very amateur performance indeed by the leading man—lacking verve, style and expertise.'

'You can't believe——' In desperation the words came, but too late.

'Relax, sweetheart. It's time you learned the difference between the boys and the men. Remember that night we first met in Sydney? Outside your unit? You didn't exactly smack my face, did you? Well, now I'm going to show you just how it should be done.'

His hand threaded through her tangle of hair, lifting her face gently so that he could stare down into it. For a few seconds his eyes dwelt on her large-pupilled eyes, the slight quivering of her softly parted lips, then, with an agonising slowness, he lowered his gold-flecked, dark brown head and kissed her.

Afterwards she realised that she'd been well fore-warned and had had all the time in the world to forearm herself either with words or actions—and she'd done neither. Perhaps it was the knowledge of her own sluggish lack of action which held her transfixed in his arms as he gathered her closer to his firm body. His mouth was sweet and soft on her own, gentle as a butterfly's wing, touching, enjoying, flirting, but never invasive until that unforgivable moment when she felt the tip of his tongue trace the long, sweeping bow of her upper lip and she caught it between her teeth, nibbling gently at it.

The next thing she knew Mel had deepened the kiss, possessing her mouth with a strength of purpose that had her clinging to his shoulders for support, as her breasts tingled in shock.

When he released her they were both panting.

For five seconds Kerry's hazel eyes blazed at his, some part of her mind registering that instead of grey they now appeared almost entirely black. In fact his whole face had changed subtly in some indefinable way, so that she had a terrible, unspeakable longing to reach out her hand and trace its outline. Horrified at the turmoil of emotion she was experiencing, she swung up her right arm and struck him hard with the palm of her hand on one lean cheek.

Apart from the narrowing of his eyes, her blow seemed to have had little effect, as he raised his left hand to touch the mark of impact.

'It seems I did somewhat better than your compatriot. I don't recollect his getting such a response,' he remarked equably. 'I think I shall take that as a sign of encouragement. Something to build on in the coming weeks.'

'You forget I'm on holiday for the next two weeks.' Kerry's palm still tingled from contact with his cheek, accusing her with its discomfort, but she wouldn't apologise. He'd deserved everything he'd got, and it wasn't as if she'd hit him that hard. It was just that his cheek was weather-beaten and her hand wasn't!

'I promise you I haven't, sweetheart.' His smile would
have put the Cheshire cat's to shame. 'It's some time
since I was last on Dunk. Believe me, I'm really looking
forward to the next fourteen days.'

CHAPTER FIVE

'But— but. . .' Anxiously Kerry searched Mel's composed face for a hint that he was taunting her. 'You're not going to Dunk. You've got to take the next tour back to Sydney!'

'Wrong, Kerry.' There was a sparkle now in his eyes which showed her just how much he was enjoying this. 'I've had a relief-driver flown up from Melbourne. As soon as you told me you and Nick Albioni had planned a holiday on Dunk I realised that his accommodation would be vacant, so I phoned him and asked him if I could take it off his hands.'

Aware that he was watching her face very carefully, trying to read her response to his bombshell, Kerry made a supreme effort to keep her dismay to a minimum, as he moved his shoulders in a lazy shrug.

'He was delighted,' he said. 'Seems he hadn't taken the precaution of taking out an insurance.'

'I see.' She swallowed hard, trying to collect her thoughts. Just when she thought she was going to be able to shake off the stress of the last two weeks, she now discovered she was going to take a large part of the cause of it with her! For the first time she truly regretted having slapped Mel McKinley's face, however much he'd asked for it. 'Well, I suppose Dunk is large enough for us to be able to avoid each other,' she said at last.

'I'm sure it is,' he agreed pleasantly. 'If that's what we both want.'

As a parting remark it didn't have a lot going for it, Kerry decided, gritting her teeth in frustration, as he sauntered towards the door, the quintessential male— powerful, graceful and totally committed to his own pleasure. Too late now to change her plans. She had paid fully for her accommodation and all meals, and although, unlike Nick, she was insured, she'd need a better excuse than incompatability with one of the other guests to claim it!

Dear heavens—talk about a thorn in her side! No man she had ever met had been able to get beneath her skin the way he did.

Leaving the bathroom and closing the door behind her, she re-entered the bedroom, sat down before the dressing-table mirror, and dragged a brush through her hair, still fuming. The worst thing of all was the effect he had on her metabolism, disturbing her senses so that at times she felt like an inexperienced teenager rather than a mature woman of twenty-two.

'Oh!' She banged the hairbrush down on the melamine surface in despair. She'd just have to make sure she saw the wretched man as little as possible in the coming days. She stared at her reflected image, raising a finger to touch her mouth. Why had Colin's kiss left her untouched, when Mel's had turned her to a quivering jelly?

For the first time in her life she felt vulnerable to a man's desire, and that could be fatal both to her pride and her peace of mind, because there had been nothing genuine about Mel's contemptuous kiss. How could there have been when he'd marked her down as a home-breaker?

Sighing, Kerry gathered up the dollar notes which she'd dropped earlier, making them into a neat pile and placing them on the bedside table. She was too tired to make a decision about them now. Tomorrow would do. Unbuttoning her dress, she laid it carefully on the bed, following it with her scanty underclothes. Naked, she walked towards the bathroom and, opening the door, recoiled from the cloud of steam which billowed out to meet her. Damn! The mixer-tap must have been turned on to full heat, and she hadn't noticed. Taking a deep breath so as to avoid inhaling the boiling steam, she walked gingerly into the room, and reached blindly to turn off the tap.

Well, she decided sourly, the bath would have to wait a while until the atmosphere cleared and she could add some cold water to the tub. Fortunately that shouldn't take long, especially since she'd turned the air conditioning on to full before going down to dinner.

Reaching for the bath-towel, she draped it round her, as a sudden jarring ringing sent her speedily back into the bedroom. Like some maniacal alarm-clock the sound pierced the stillness of the early morning. Panic-stricken because in a moment other guests would surely complain, Kerry dropped on her knees beside the radio console by the side of her bed. Oh, dear heavens, this was all she needed! Near to tears, she sought to discover some fiendish alarm which had inadvertently been set off. Nothing!

'Please,' she murmured, turning her eyes to heaven and clasping her hands. 'Oh, please, can't you do something?'

Never had a prayer been answered so quickly. Before the last word had been spoken a spray of fine but incessant water gushed down from various points across the entire ceiling. Her eyes wide with horror, Kerry could only gasp unbelievingly as the unremitting shower soaked everything in the room, including herself.

When she heard the rush of running footsteps down the corridor, immediately followed by the sound of a key rasping in her door, she was beyond words, clutching the now soaking towel around herself as the night manager burst into the room followed by two men carrying fire extinguishers. It was only when she saw Mel McKinley stride into view behind them, his face more stern than the masks of Melanesian war gods, that the situation finally defeated her. Sinking down on the sopping bed, she burst into tears.

There were less than a dozen people in the sunlit departure lounge of Cairns Airport waiting for the morning flight to Dunk. Kerry, dressed in a pale lemon, capped-sleeved cotton dress, with a wide picot-edged neckline, regarded her pretty tan sandals with a sombre regard. What an inauspicious way to end her first tour of the tropics! As she had guessed last night, her experience had been given wide coverage around the hotel, and she'd had to run the gauntlet of good-humoured teasing from several members of the staff as well as her passengers! She shivered. If she lived to be a hundred she'd never forget the look on Mel's face as he'd stormed into her sodden bedroom. But to date he'd been the only one to refrain from mentioning the incident.

'Hi, Kerry!'

The object of her thoughts, dressed in his cyclone-survival T-shirt over tan shorts, took the seat beside her, stretching out his long legs.

'Well, I must say you look a lot drier now than when I saw you last night!' He angled her an oblique look.

Embarrassed by her own stupidity, she stayed silent. At least he didn't appear to be as angry as she'd anticipated. She'd been expecting a right dressing down for the chaos she'd unwittingly caused. Especially if the look on his face the previous night had been anything to go by!

'I suppose you realise how it happened?' Laughter thickened his deep voice as she sighed, prepared to endure his mockery.

'Yes, the security guys told me. Because I left the air conditioning on to maximum the temperature in the bedroom was so low that when the steam from the bathroom escaped it was channelled upwards into the heat sensors, and automatically set the sprays working.'

'You sure like a hot bath, sweetheart!' He looked at her curiously. 'What were you up to—extorting some kind of penance from yourself for your sins?'

'What sins?' she asked tartly. 'No, if you must know, you made me so angry that I forgot to check whether the tap was mixing correctly.'

'A little kiss and you flood a hotel?' The grey eyes were warm. 'You're a dangerous lady, Kerry. I wonder what you would have done if I'd seduced you?'

'Ruined your future chances of doing the same to anyone else!' she retorted fiercely. Then she felt her own mouth quiver as her sense of humour rose to overcome the shame of her humiliation. 'I suppose there is a funny side to it,' she admitted. 'Perhaps when I'm old and grey I'll be able to make my grandchildren laugh with a detailed account of how Granny went to take a bath and awakened a whole hotel in the small hours of the morning.'

She glanced away, unable to meet his clear grey gaze as her mind was invaded by the unwelcome memory that if Murray could have his way they'd be Mel's grandchildren as well.

'You do yourself an injustice, Kerry. I reckon you'll be laughing about it within forty-eight hours. If it's any consolation to you, you're not the first person to set the alarms off by mistake.'

'Believe me, I won't make the same error again!' Her expression grew serious. 'To be honest, when I saw your face last night I thought you were going to fire me on the spot to preserve the good name of the company.'

'And alienate you when I'm looking forward to enjoying your company for the next couple of weeks?' he demanded smoothly. 'That would have been a very short-sighted action. Besides, you're mistaking concern for anger.'

He allowed his eyes to dwell on her defiant face. 'I was at the reception desk checking with the night clerk that

all late bills for extras had been prepared for our party
when the alarm went off and your room number lit up. I
had a sudden vision of your having decided to set fire to
the bundle of notes I'd given you as a grand gesture of
rejection, and finding the resulting conflagration beyond
your power to control. Believe me, I wasn't looking
forward to telling Murray that his granddaughter had
become a human sacrifice in the cause of independence.'

'You mean you're reserving judgement?' Kerry didn't
trust his smoothness one little bit. Neither did she want
to spend the next few days wondering if she still had a
job.

'Judgement?' His smile mocked her. 'You expect some
kind of verdict from me?'

'Why not?' she challenged. 'You made it quite clear
from the start that I was on trial!'

'Just normal staff assessment.' Mel gave her a sharp
look. 'Let's say that I wasn't prepared to accept either
Murray's or Albioni's estimations of your capabilities. I
felt both could be—how shall I say it—prejudiced?'

'And now?' Childlike she crossed her fingers hidden
in the lemon cotton of her dress, wanting his approval
for her own pride and Murray's satisfaction, and knowing that, despite his earlier dismissal of it, last night's
escapade must have added a black mark to her report—
or should she say a damp mark?

He subjected her to an appraisal so searching that the
warm blood tingled in her cheeks and she felt more
naked than she had the previous evening with only a
soggy towel to protect her modesty. 'Well, no one could
dispute your charm and friendliness, your capacity for
hard work and your enduring politeness under duress—
to the passengers, that is,' he amended silkily. 'Your
paperwork and appearance are faultless too, but you do
seem to lack a sense of discipline.'

'Armies run on discipline!' She tossed her head arro-
gantly, feeling the russet waves bounce on her shoulders
as she found it impossible to conceal her resentment.

'So does McKinleys,' he returned softly. 'Doing what you're told in an emergency without question can save lives.'

'And you think I wouldn't?' she asked fiercely.

Mel shrugged. 'I'm saying you appear to provide your own translation of the company rules at times.'

'If you're still on about Colin,' she began heatedly, 'it was he who——'

'As a matter of fact I was thinking of the day you spent out on the Reef when you didn't feel the need to wear your uniform all the time.' His eyebrows lifted interrogatively, inviting an explanation.

Kerry drew her breath in with a little hiss, instantly recalling her pleasure at being able to relax away from his overbearing vigilance the day she had escorted the passengers to a coral cay several miles from the coast while he had spent the time in Cairns supervising the servicing of their coach.

'I didn't realise you'd set up a spy system to monitor my misdeeds, but yes, you're quite right. I'd never been snorkelling before, and I'm afraid the temptation proved too much for me.' Her eyes sparkled with antagonism as she added, 'I hope your informer was suitably rewarded?'

Mel shook his head, refuting her allegation. 'As a matter of fact, several of our party went out of their way to tell me what a pretty girl you were and how lovely you looked in your swimsuit.'

Oh, dear heavens! Was there a conspiracy afoot to sing her praises to this irritating man? Couldn't anyone see they had nothing in common?

'Since at least half the passengers were snorkelling too,' she defended herself strongly, 'I thought my presence among them—suitably clad—would be quite appropriate. Besides, it seems to me that several of the rules applying to staff are antiquated and could do with being rescinded.'

Mel regarded her, a strange glint reflected in his sombre eyes.

'I just bet it does, sweetheart, and I wouldn't take odds against which ones,' he returned softly. 'But that kind of decision comes from the top.'

'Rather than the people operating in the front line, you mean?' Kerry knew he had a legitimate point and she was putting words into his mouth, but somehow reason seemed to flee when she was close to him. 'If you feel like that about it I'll resign now and save you the trouble of cataloguing all my faults officially!'

'And find your own way back to Sydney?' he asked mildly. 'You seem to have forgotten you're travelling back there courtesy of Metline as hostess on the next Cairns/Sydney tour in two weeks' time.'

Her heart sank. He was right. She couldn't afford to resign until she was back south.

His smile recognised her surrender, and she responded to his perception with a mixture of fierce antagonism and an equally vivid sense of inexplicable excitement, as he leaned towards her.

He said softly, 'One of the lessons you need to learn, Kerry, is that you can't win them all. You may be able to make Murray dance to your tune, but you'll find I'm not so easily impressed by spoiled young women who think that they can get what they want with a flick of their skirts and a toss of their heads, and tough luck to anyone who stands in their way!'

Kerry's mouth opened in astonishment, as words failed her. He was talking about her? Accusing her of some nameless sin against her grandfather whom she loved and whom she was sure loved her in return? She stared back at Mel's handsome face, the pulse at the base of her throat hammering with agitation, and read in his steady gaze not only the condemnation she had expected, but also a challenge that she prove him wrong.

A cold fear held her motionless. She should leave now;

pick up her hand luggage and leave the airport; phone Murray, borrow the return air fare to Sydney; leave Cairns; but most of all leave Mel McKinley—because every instinct told her he was aching for a show-down with her. She didn't know what about or why, but if and when it came she surmised she would have very little chance of surviving it whole.

At the moment her limbs unfroze and she would have made her move he glanced away from her towards the glass exit-doors leading to the runway, seemingly unaware of the effect his words had had on her.

It was now or never. But cowardice had never been one of her failings, and why should she be cheated out of her holiday? A second thought struck her, causing her stiff mouth to relax. Perhaps she was over-reacting? Perhaps Mel's outburst, with its overtones of bitterness, had been aimed at Belinda Fraser and not her at all? Incongruously, disappointment in love was one thing they shared. Mel's relationship with Belinda had foundered, and hers with Nick Albioni had never got off the ground. The irony was that she had Mel's arbitrary judgement to thank for the heartache and remorse she had been spared. Suppose Nick had been able to come with her, and had continued to deceive her? She shuddered, contemplating the fool she might have made of herself.

'Well? Coming or not?' A cynical sparkle illuminated Mel's eyes, and it was impossible not to be aware of their challenge, as if he had read her secret thoughts, knew the powerful extent of her reservations and was enjoying her mental battle. How could she cancel all her long-looked-forward-to plans and accord him such an easy victory?

'Coming,' she said smoothly, and even managed a smile.

Seated in the small two-engined inter-island plane a few minutes later, she turned her face from the window to glance at the strong profile next to her. Mel's head was lowered over an in-flight magazine, his golden, fuzzed thigh a warm, disturbing presence against her own. She eased away, but had to admit that the lack of space made complete avoidance impossible. Still, it was only a short flight, and she supposed that she could tolerate the claustrophobic atmosphere his dominating presence exercised on her for three-quarters of an hour.

Nevertheless it was a deep sense of relief she felt as the plane landed smoothly on Dunk's small runway. The aerial view of the island as they'd made their descent had already confirmed Murray's description of heaven on earth. She had even found it an effort to make out the low cabanas of the resort along Brammo Bay, sprinkled as they were among a garden which still kept most of its rainforest inheritance. She'd glimpsed wide sweeps of deserted beaches lapped by a turquoise sea of incredible clarity and thick, verdant, virgin rainforest, culminating in the green summit of Mount Kootaloo, and she was raring to enjoy this long-awaited holiday. No one and nothing was going to spoil her happiness, she decided firmly.

A glowing excitement possessed her as she reached the small, canopied reception area which served as Dunk's airport building, where she accepted a glass of orange juice and champagne from one of the waiting resort hostesses. Murray had told her Dunk and the other islands in its family group were virtually unspoiled, three-quarters of the main island being gazetted as a National Park, but even then she hadn't dared to hope for anything quite so perfect.

'Peaceful isn't it?' Mel came across to join her, a glass in his hand. 'One of the things I appreciate most about this place is the lack of traffic noise.'

'Yes,' Kerry nodded, registering the fact that it wasn't his first visit. 'Murray told me there aren't any proper roads, and the only vehicles which use the larger tracks are the resort trucks and the airport minibus. How big is the island?'

'Oh, about six kilometres long and two wide at its widest part, but the measurements are deceptive because it's all too easy to get lost in dense rainforest unless you keep to the marked tracks, and it's quite impossible to walk round the whole island in a day—so don't try it! Another thing,' he continued inexorably. 'If you're going out for a walk, make sure you give yourself plenty of time to get back to the resort. We're in the tropics now and the evenings are very short—and there aren't any streetlights to guide you back to your cabana!'

'Thank you.' Kerry contrived to look grateful as she fought down a sense of irritation. What did he think she was—six years old?

'You resent my advice?' Apparently she hadn't been successful in aping gratitude. 'My dear Kerry, I'm just ensuring that your relatively short stay in the tropics won't prove hazardous to your health. As I understand it, this lucky land has a few natural hazards you won't find in Europe.' Abruptly he changed the subject before she could point out tartly that she'd seen both releases of *Crocodile Dundee*. 'Has your case been unloaded from the plane?'

'Yes, it's over there.' She pointed to the pile of luggage about to be loaded into a small truck.

'Good. Then we can go. I've collected the key from the hostess, and the cabana's only a short walk from here. We don't need a lift.'

Muttering a little under her breath at the easy way he continued to assume control, Kerry duly followed as he led the way down a short path, over a small bridge and into the gardens of the resort.

Only a few minutes later he stopped on the covered veranda outside a cabana, one of a block of four, surrounded by papaya bushes, jasmine and Brazilian torch lilies.

'This is it.' He turned the key in the lock, sliding the glass door open, and standing back for her to enter.

'Oh, how lovely! Isn't it big?' Delighted, Kerry took in the two double beds, the table and two free-standing chairs, the coffee-making facilities, the curtained wardrobe and the two enormous, slow-moving fans which revolved above her head.

'Everything we need,' he agreed smoothly. 'See, the bathroom's through here.'

For the first time a qualm of anxiety stilled Kerry's euphoria. Instead of following him to the bathroom door to inspect the layout of the room, she remained where she was, feeling an unpleasant increase in her pulse.

'This is *my* cabana isn't it?' she asked levelly.

'Ours, sweetheart.' He seemed in no way disturbed by the outrageous statement he'd just made. 'Yup! I think we're going to be very comfortable here.'

'Mel. . .' Kerry took a deep breath, her senses reeling. 'I don't think you quite understood me. Where will you be sleeping?'

'Makes no difference to me.' He shrugged broad shoulders. 'You choose which bed you prefer.'

'You imagine you're sharing this cabana with me?' Her eyes flashed a furious fire into his bland face. 'This is ridiculous! How dare you suppose——?'

'Don't lose your temper with me, sweetheart!' Three long strides had brought him to her side. 'You've had plenty enough time to make your feelings known since last night. If you didn't like the idea, *then* was the time to say so. I might, and I repeat *might* even have been prepared to listen to you up to the time the plane took off. Now it's too late, and all your sham innocence is going to get you nowhere.' His voice was harsh, his eyes narrowed as he glared down at her from his superior height.

'And just exactly how was I supposed to know what you had in mind?' she demanded angrily.

'You can't be that dim, surely, Kerry,' he snarled. 'I told you I'd taken over Nick Albioni's accommodation. At the time you didn't go into hysterics of maidenly modesty.'

'Because Nick and I weren't going to share a cabana!'

'Save the play-acting. It won't wash,' he retorted grimly, holding up a hand to silence her as she would have protested. 'Albioni himself told me all about your plans.'

'What?' The blood drained from Kerry's face. 'That's impossible. Nick and I——'

'Were "just good friends". Yeah, I know that, darling. You've told me that story so many times I'm beginning to think you believe it yourself. If you're trying to stop your lover being sacked for disobeying the company's non-fraternisation rules for drivers and hostesses, forget it. Unfortunately for both of you, when I got Nick cornered he had no alternative but to tell me he couldn't sell me his holiday because you and he were sharing a cabana. Luckily for his financial well-being, I didn't see that as an impediment to the deal.'

'He was lying!'

'Sure looks like it.' Mel allowed his eyes to wander around the room as Kerry stood silent, fighting a sudden desire to scream in frustration. There was no way Mel McKinley was going to believe a word of her denial, and as for Nick! Some friend he had turned out to be, deliberately lying to her about his plans. A wave of nausea engulfed her. It would have been bad enough if Nick had merely intended to take a holiday away from his wife in her company—but his plans had been a lot more devious than that! And who would believe how green she had been? Certainly not her cynical, contemptuous companion.

He had already made it clear that he saw her as a parasite and manipulator, and now, despite her protestations of innocence, the double cabana not only confirmed his opinion of her low moral values, but her innocent silence about it had also suggested she wasn't particular about sharing it with him!

All the time she'd been comforting herself that at least if she couldn't prove she hadn't known Nick was married, their occupation of separate cabanas would have substantiated her claim that they'd never been more than friends; and now the evidence had turned against her!

'But—but if you believed what he said, why did you decide to come here? You must have known I wouldn't dream of sharing with you?'

'Must I have?' To her horror Mel reached out one lazy hand to grasp her chin, forcing her head backwards so that he could gaze down into her wide eyes. 'On the contrary, I had very great hopes that you would accept a change of partners with your customary sanguinity, and you've still got to persuade me I'm wrong. Hell, Kerry!' He abandoned her chin, but remained dominating her by his height and nearness. 'There's not much fun in being alone in paradise, is there? And after all, you're no shy virgin, are you? Neither did you exactly grimace with horror when I kissed you outside your unit, did you?' It was said with such smugness that Kerry's voice locked in her throat. 'As for your little protest in Cairns, I imagine that was because I'd caught you and Colin in each other's arms, and spoiled your fun, hmm?'

Amusement and some less easily defined emotion curdled the timbre of his voice.

'I promise I can turn in a better performance than your young compatriot any day! So shall we take the conventional protests as read, and make the most of our time together?'

Oh! If there were only something to hand with which she could wipe that smile off his handsome face! Words were useless against his adamantine prejudice.

'Don't try it,' he warned gently, his smile deepening. 'You got away with it last time because I'm not vindictive by nature, but there's a limit to the number of slaps I'll allow you to land before retaliating—and my palm's a lot harder than yours.' He smiled, but it wasn't ingratiating, more anticipatory, as if the prospect of slapping her would give him some pleasure.

'Come on, Kerry,' he continued. 'You've put up a sturdy defence, but it's not fooling anyone, and I'm getting bored with your protestations of girlish innocence. I'm no indulgent grandfather to be blinded by an enchanting smile and a delectable body, but on the other hand I can offer you a warm and rewarding relationship for the next two weeks; so why don't you give in gracefully?'

His dark brown head tipped interrogatively as his eyes laughed at her. 'Like you said, the cabana's large enough, and I'm a caring and considerate room-mate. Besides, since I've deprived you of your lover's company, the least I can do is try to compensate for his absence. Relax. It could be fun. You may even find I have other advantages over Nick Albioni, apart from the obvious one—that I happen to be unmarried.'

CHAPTER SIX

SINCE it was no use continuing to protest her total ignorance of Nick's plans, in the face of Mel's patent disbelief, Kerry must try to attack him on another plane.

'There's one rule for you and another for other drivers and hostesses, you mean?' she asked, her voice sharp with sarcasm as she hoped to shame him.

He sighed patiently. 'That's a policy to ensure that passengers aren't embarrassed by overt displays of affection or lovers' feuds between two people to whom they've entrusted their well-being. And the reason it doesn't apply to us any more is that I'm no longer a driver. I've already arranged for a relief-man to be flown up from Sydney for the next tour leaving Cairns for the return journey.'

'You think of everything, don't you?' she snapped.

'I try.'

His smug reply incensed her.

'Well, this is the second time in a row you've backed a loser, Mr McKinley!' She heaved in a deep breath in an effort to quiet the racing of her heart as the adrenalin pumped round her system.

'Second?' he drawled, with raised eyebrows.

'I understand Belinda Fraser wasn't impressed with what you had to offer, either.'

At any other time she would have been ashamed of repeating gossip to one of the parties concerned; now she felt justified in using any weapon which came to hand.

She hadn't anticipated the slow smile which greeted her sally, or the way his mouth would turn, displaying small elongated lines at its corners.

'Thank you for pointing out that we have something

else in common. Both of us have been let down by our lovers. Why shouldn't we console each other?'

It was more than Kerry could bear. What point would there be in protesting her total innocence, not only of Nick but of men in general in a carnal sense? Mel McKinley had attributed her with sharing his own loose moral code, and nothing was going to dissuade him that she was more sinned against than sinning. There was only one way left.

'Because I'm discriminating,' she said coldly. 'And you're just not my type.'

'Perhaps I could be.' He held her attention with eyes which seemed to have discovered some hypnotic power. 'Why not give me the chance to convince you, Kerry?'

She should have been prepared, but when he made his move towards her it took her by surprise. She had been girding herself for verbal battle, not physical contact, so that when his arms gathered her to his strong form and he released one hand to tip her chin upwards she had no immediate defence ready.

His kiss was sweet and demanding, hard enough to shock her but not hard enough to hurt, other than to leave her soft lips tingling with its pressure as she found some latent strength at last to oppose him, and he let her go.

Without a word she backed away from him, then turned abruptly, heading for the door. She was trembling, her mind a turmoil of emotions, frightened not so much by Mel's uncompromising ardour but by her own reaction to it. For she was horribly, excitingly aware that given the opportunity he might very well convince her that he *was* her type—to her everlasting shame!

'Wait!' Harshly his voice accosted her. 'Where are you going?'

'I'm leaving Dunk this minute.' Kerry's voice shook as her fingers sought the catch of the sliding-doors.

'How?' There was no anger in the lazy query. 'There's

no more flights today, the ferry's already left, and even if you could get the water-taxi back to Mission Beach, what would you do when you got there? No money, no hotel accommodation? Where would you go, Kerry?'

All his points were valid, but she wouldn't waver, as her active brain sought a solution. 'I'll camp on the island, then!'

'Not without a permit, you won't, and you can be sure the limited number available have all been issued months ago.'

'Perhaps there's another cabana vacant. . .' Desperation echoed in her reply.

'Wishful thinking, sweetheart. This place is a Mecca in the winter for tired Melbourne businessmen. They queue up six deep to get a bed.' Mel sighed with deliberate exaggeration. 'Square up to facts, Kerry. You and I are going to be cabana-mates for the next fourteen days. It shouldn't be so bad; none of the other ladies I've had the pleasure of sharing a room with has ever accused me of snoring.'

'Bully for you!' At the end of her tether, Kerry was close to tears of sheer exasperation, but no way was she going to let him get the last word.

Apprehensive about her tangled feelings and the havoc he could cause to her metabolism, she was determined more than ever that she wouldn't allow him to crush her spirit. If she had to remain on the island she would continue to fight him and oppose him with any argument she could manufacture, since he wouldn't listen to reason.

'In that case it seems you may be getting the worst of the bargain,' she told him with assumed sweetness, totally abandoning the truth in her furious impotency. 'All my past lovers have complained bitterly and at length about the noise I make!'

Not waiting for his response, she slid the door to one side, making her exit at great speed through the ensuing opening. Space—that was what she needed; and time to think! Walking a few steps forward, she found herself confronting the cascade-pool, where two people were idly swimming while others sat sunbathing, drinking long, cool drinks from the bar, or reading in idyllic surroundings. Having no idea where she was heading, she glimpsed a high roof over the flowering shrubs and made towards it. In a few moments she had found the main reception office and enormous lounge and dining-room, with its open-sided aspect to the rainforest. At least she could check Mel's allegation about Nick's booking!

Fifteen minutes later she was forced to accept he had been speaking the truth. Not only about Nick's under-handedness, but about the resort being fully booked.

Making her way into the cool, deserted lounge, she sank down into one of the large and deeply cushioned cane armchairs. She'd been a fool. But no one, least of all the self-opinionated chairman of McKinleys, was going to believe that she could have been so innocent at her age. That was what happened when you took people at their face value!

Damn all men! Kerry pushed her hair away from her forehead, a tense nervous action which betrayed the tumult within her. All she'd wanted was to do a good job, and that had meant being friendly, smiling, helpful to everyone who requested it. It had also included playing a supportive role to Nick Albioni in the first instance and Mel McKinley in the second! In neither instances had it required her to go to bed with either of them!

Doubtless Mel would be astonished if he were ever to discover just how uninterested she had been in forming liaisons of the emotional kind. On the whole, although she genuinely liked the male sex, intrigued by the way they reasoned differently from women, fascinated by the polarity of their interests—the way that when several of them got together the conversation inevitably turned to

sport or cars—it didn't mean she had her mind fixed on
marriage, or went weak at the knees every time she saw
a baby. Unlike many of her female friends, she had
never looked on every new boyfriend as a potential
husband, neither had she wanted to squander her latent
emotions by indulging in experimental affairs with young
men she had liked only as friends.

Nor had she ever felt unfulfilled or deprived by the
lack of a lover, having been more than contented with
the demands of her chosen career in hotel management,
and her wide circle of friends of both sexes, until the day
she had made her momentous decision to travel halfway
around the world in search of her heritage.

Then Nick had entered her life and she'd realised that
not only had she enjoyed his company and been flattered
by his discreet attention towards her, but she had also
found him physically attractive in a way that other men
had left her unmoved. She had neither loved him nor
been in love with him, but she had cared enough about
him to want to give their relationship time to mature,
away from the calls to duty which had hitherto surrounded it. But she hadn't intended to force that matur-
ation by sharing a cabana with him, and she had made
that point perfectly clear to him at the time. Her decision
hadn't precluded the eventuality that they might become
lovers—but it certainly hadn't anticipated it!

That was what made Mel McKinley's harsh judgement
of her so totally unbearable. Yet why should she allow
him to ruin a holiday she'd been looking forward to ever
since Murray had delineated the joys of Dunk and
suggested she arrange her tour of duty to coincide with a
break there?

No, she wouldn't run away like a frightened rabbit,
she decided sturdily. She'd stay and fight him every inch
of the way. Whatever his sins—and she imagined them
to be manifold—his stated aim was seduction, not
coercion.

Sighing deeply, she stretched out her legs, feeling some of the tension draining from her. A plan of action was firming up in her mind. She would stay on Dunk, and tonight she would take the two chairs from the cabana and make herself a makeshift bed outside on the ground-level veranda, just to show him how determined she was not to share the room with him! Hopefully, when he realised how resolute she was, he would cut his losses and return to the mainland and leave her in peace!

Having formed a plan of action, Kerry felt a great deal better. Leaving the pleasant solitude of the lounge, she sauntered outside, and skirted the rectangular hibiscus pool on the terrace to step directly on to the silver sand of the fabulous Bramma Bay. There were less than a dozen people on the whole coconut-tree-fringed beach, and she caught her breath at the sheer beauty of the scene before her. The almost motionless Coral Sea gleamed like watered turquoise silk beneath the cloudless sky, and in the distance she could see the coast of mainland Australia.

If only she'd changed into a swimsuit, she thought ruefully, or had had time to apply sunscreen to her sensitive skin; but her suitcase hadn't arrived by the time she'd stormed out of the cabana, and it was too soon to return there. Mel would see it as a sign of surrender, and she had no wish for a further confrontation. Deciding to compromise, she dragged a white slatted beach-lounger beneath the shade of a coconut palm and, sprawling out on it, closed her eyes and gave herself up to the pleasures of warmth and silence.

'Hi! I thought I might find you here. Impressive, isn't it?'

There was no mistaking Mel's deep voice as she struggled from her comatose state to look at her watch, surprised to find out that more than two hours had elapsed since she'd last set eyes on him. She stretched luxuriously, feeling good. She must have cat-napped, and it had certainly soothed her jaded nerves.

'I've been renewing old acquaintances,' he continued pleasantly, obviously not expecting an answer to a purely rhetorical question as he hunkered down on the sand beside her, taking a handful of it in his lean fist and allowing it to trickle out between his fingers.

'When were you last here?' she asked politely, deciding that her future policy would be one of cool courtesy, since verbal fighting seemed to stimulate the worst in his nature.

'A couple of years before my father died. We'd come up to Cairns to inspect some new rolling-stock we had on order. There was some problem about meeting the delivery date, and we decided if we were going to have to hang around in the tropics here would be as good a place as any.'

'Has it changed much?'

'Not that I've seen.' His tone was abrupt enough to make Kerry's eyebrows rise. 'Look, Kerry, can we call a truce? Fate seems to have decided we're spending this holiday in each other's company, and we'll both enjoy it a great deal more if we can be civil to each other.'

Biting back the retort which sprang to her lips—that it was McKinley himself, not Fate, who had forced such an unhappy destiny on her—Kerry maintained her air of coolness with considerable effort.

'I thought I *was* being civil,' she said innocently.

'No, you didn't, sweetheart,' he corrected her crisply, his eyes narrowed against the glare of the sun as he called her bluff. 'You were being deliberately distant.'

'Then why not find a companion who suits your mood better than I do?' she suggested amiably, not in the least astonished by his percipience.

'Because *you* are the companion I want, and if your mood doesn't suit me, then I intend to do my best to change it.'

'You're welcome to try.' She shrugged her shoulders dismissively, but a small curl of heat unfolded inside her at his uncompromising statement.

'Good! I hope you remember that invitation tonight?' His voice was low and quiet, sharp as pointed steel, penetrating her composure as he propped himself on one elbow to lean over her.

Wanting only to escape, Kerry tried to scramble off the lounger, her feet not getting a firm grip in the shifting sand.

'Here, take my hand.' Mel had experienced no such difficulty in rising quickly from his recumbent position to offer her his large, masculine hand.

Then, as she hesitated, he grasped her reluctant palm, pulling her upright in one smooth movement, releasing his hold as soon as she was standing.

'All right, then.' Kerry faced him, her eyes bright with controlled temper. 'I agree with you that we can't keep airing our differences in front of other people during our stay here, and I agree to a truce provided you promise that under no circumstances will you force your. . .your unwelcome attentions on me!'

She didn't need to see the cleft in his chin deepen as Mel made a vain attempt to hide his amusement.

'By that quaint Victorian expression I assume you mean that I won't seduce you against your will?' he mused softly. 'Yes, yes, I think I can give you that undertaking. And now that's settled, how about a spot of lunch?'

Kerry wasn't so dumb that she didn't realise that what he was saying was that he would take no for an answer, but beneath his declaration was the subliminal suggestion that the time would come when she would cease to say no. Let him think he had won the point. She knew herself a lot better than he did!

'Lunch sounds lovely,' she told him honestly.

From a large selection of cold meats and fish, tropical

salads and resort-baked bread displayed in the large
dining-room, Kerry helped herself to slices of smoked
salmon, some king prawns, a chunk of fresh lemon and
slices of brown bread with butter, carrying them outside
at Mel's suggestion.

They ate at a small table, cool beneath a large blue
and white sun-umbrella with the hibiscus pool on one
side of them and the beach on the other, washing down
their repast with a light Australian beer.

Perhaps it was the idyllic setting, or the delicious food,
but suddenly Kerry found Mel's presence not only
acceptable, but almost welcome. It was a strange feeling,
and one that needed some investigation, she thought,
delicately shelling the last of the enormous prawns.

Divorced from the friction which had existed between
them from their very first meeting, he possessed many
of the qualities she admired in a man, she admitted. He
had a strength of character which equalled his physical
capabilities, he was hard-working, prepared to accept
responsibility, and had shown a sense of humour
throughout the tour, except perhaps where she was
concerned! The passengers had certainly found him an
attractive personality, and to do him justice his caring
attitude towards them had seemed natural and unforced.

Perhaps if they'd met under any other circumstances
they might even have liked each other. That was one of
the things she'd never understood about men—how they
could separate desire from love, how it was possible for
a man to make love to a woman he neither knew nor
liked if the mood was on him. For her, and for most
women, she suspected, physical attraction would never
be enough. And Mel McKinley was very physically
attractive indeed!

Finishing her meal, Kerry placed her knife and fork
neatly on the plate, and raised her eyes to scan his face
as he sat opposite her, gazing over the pool. Watching

the lissom Australian beauties who were . . .
it?

Feature by feature he was nothing extraor
there was something about his face which caugh
heart and brought a wild beating to her pulse. Ab
really, she scolded herself. Nick was far more handsome
in his dark Latin way, yet he had never aroused such
turbulent sensations when she had looked at him—and
why was it impossible for her to forget the occasions on
which Mel had kissed her? Angry, contemptuous salutes,
all of them—so why did she continue to wonder what it
would be like to be kissed by him when he really meant
it?

'A dollar for your thoughts.' His hands reached across
the table to cover her own.

'They're not worth it!' Quickly she gave the traditional
response, furious when she felt herself blushing. Why
hadn't she realised that his attention was no longer fixed
on the pool?

'No?' His smile challenged her.

'It was the tide,' she improvised rapidly. 'I was looking
past your shoulder at the sea, and I realised just how
much it had gone out. I can see where the smooth sand
ends and lumps of small rocks break the surface.'

'That's because we're so far along the bay.' Thankfully
he followed her lead, but his eyes continued to contest
her explanation. 'Down further by the jetty there's
always plenty of deep water. But if you continue past
that and cross the sandspit you'll come to another beach
called Pallon. Dunk and the family islands are the peaks
of a submerged continental shelf and when it's low tide
it's possible to walk across the sand to Mung-um-
gnackum Island from Pallon Beach.'

'That has to be an aboriginal name!' Eagerly Kerry
leaned forward, her face aglow with interest, her reservations temporarily in abeyance in her search for knowledge. 'Murray told me that Dunk's aboriginal name was

Coonanglebah, which meant Island of Peace and Plenty, but he never mentioned Mung-um-gnackum. Do you know what it means?'

'Not for certain, although local opinion has it that actually it's an aboriginal swear-word. As I said, the tide goes out very fast and very far, and the story goes that it was quite common for the aborigines returning from a fishing trip to find themselves beached there, upon which they would gnash their teeth and cry out "Oh, mung-um-gnackum! Stranded again!"'

'You're making fun of me!' Kerry looked reproachful. 'OK, so I'm a naïve pommy Sheila, but if I don't ask questions, how am I going to learn?'

She leaned back in her chair, gazing at her hands clasped in her lap. 'I suppose it seems absurd to you, but I do feel very deeply about this country. After all, my father was Australian, and if he'd survived 'Nam I would have been brought up here. Of course, I love England, but that doesn't mean I can't find room in my heart for Australia, too. But I don't want to do it blindly, through instinct and in total ignorance!' She stopped, biting her lip, feeling tears burning behind her eyes.

'How discriminating you are, sweetheart.' The laughter had died from Mel's face as he leaned towards her, lowering his voice to keep their conversation intimate. 'It's a pity you don't apply such high standards for the men in your life. Devotion based on true knowledge would be a prize for any man to treasure. Wait!' He spoke peremptorily as she pushed back her chair with every intention of leaving. 'I don't want you getting the wrong impression, Kerry. I wasn't mocking you about Mung-um-gnackum; if it does have a genuine translation, I've never heard of it. And as for Albioni—forget him, Kerry! I'm sorry if you fancy yourself in love with him, but he's never going to leave his wife and children for you!'

'Thank you for the counselling.' Ice dripped from her

voice. 'To be honest with you, I never expected that he would!' It was nothing but the truth, but Mel would put his own infuriating interpretation on her statement. 'Can I go now?'

'Provided you don't have any plans for leaving Dunk.' He gazed at her from eyes slitted against the powerful rays of the sun. 'I don't want you taking off into the bush in a fit of pique, and getting lost.'

'As you pointed out, I can't leave.' She met his gaze without flinching. 'But I would like the afternoon to myself. Do you have the key to the cabana? I need to unpack.'

'Sure.' He reached into the pocket of his shorts. 'Here you are. If you've any valuables, I suggest you put them in a safety-deposit box in Reception, then we can leave the door unlocked. You'll find the guests here singularly law-abiding, and if some nefarious thief does slip in he's hardly likely to be interested in second-hand clothes.'

With a nod of thanks Kerry took the key. She'd unpack, put on shorts and some strong shoes, and go for a leisurely walk through the rainforest. She remembered seeing a booklet about the island on the table of the cabana. There were bound to be some marked walks in it.

Of course, she reasoned, enjoying a cool shower, she could make sure she got to the cabana first that evening, and lock Mel out! In her mind's eye she envisaged him banging on the door awakening their neighbours, and if she remained adamant he'd wake up Reception. She shivered. No, that would be too humiliating for words. Her original idea was still best, but if there was something better she'd find it this afternoon. What better way to find it than to commune with nature?

It was dusk when she returned to the resort. The fifteen-minute walk she'd taken had ended on a small beach known as Muggy-muggy. She'd approached it

somewhat cautiously, since the guidebook had recommended it for 'getting the kind of tan you can't show
your friends', and she hadn't wanted to embarrass a
fellow guest. But it had been deserted save for a number
of sea-birds. After exploring it and examining the variety
of strange shells that littered its sand, interspersed with
bleached white coral fronds, Kerry had found an old
bench by a picnic-table and seated herself, content to
watch the numerous sea-birds which paraded before her.

Unfortunately she'd come to no other solution about
her sleeping arrangements. An obvious alternative would
be to persuade Mel McKinley to do the gentlemanly
thing and change places with her, she thought wistfully,
realising she had more chance of *that* than Canute had
had of dismissing the waves.

The cabana was empty. Good, that gave her first
option in the bathroom. She took her time, showering
leisurely before applying make-up. When she was on
duty she'd used a minimum of make-up, preferring to
give the friendly girl-next-door appearance, since passengers seemed more comfortable with this than dealing
with a glamour-girl. Now she was under no such con-
straints. She could amuse herself with the palette of eye
colours she'd brought with her.

Mmm, not bad. She surveyed the finished product,
her mouth twitching in mischief. Since Mel McKinley
saw her as a *femme fatale*, she might just as well make
the most of what she'd got! There was one thing about
having fair colouring—applying make-up, even with
discretion, made a load of difference. Her eyes seemed
much larger, their lashes longer, and the flick of colour
she'd touched on the points of her cheekbones seemed
to have sharpened them. Only her mouth seemed the
same—soft and generously curved, its outline perfectly
balanced. No lipstick could enhance it, but the delicate
colour she applied certainly emphasised its lack of fault.
Although, staring critically in the glass, Kerry was

unaware of its perfection, more concerned in making sure there was no lipstick on her white teeth.

She covered her scant underclothes with the other dress she'd brought with her—a turquoise slub linen with shoulder-ties and a straight skirt—finishing the effect by wearing high-heeled champagne sandals on her bare feet, and spraying her neck with the expensive French perfume she'd purchased at the duty-free shop at Heathrow. For a change, her hair had decided to behave itself, and all she'd needed to do was to brush it back from her forehead, clip it each side, and allow it to fall in shiny tresses to touch her bare shoulders.

Seven o'clock, and dinner wasn't served for another half-hour. Where was Mel? she wondered. In the bar, probably. Perhaps she should go up there and order herself a pre-dinner drink? On the other hand. . .

Her machinations were terminated as a familiar figure arrived on the veranda and made its way inside.

'So you didn't get lost.' He regarded her approvingly, almost warmly, as he observed the effect of her appearance.

'Neither did you,' she returned smartly. 'Although I was beginning to think our accommodation problem had been solved.'

'Think, or hope?' he queried, regarding her closely. 'If you've got any ideas of putting a couple of funnel-webs in my bed, forget it. They'd probably bite you first, and I'm sure that's not what you had in mind! In any case, as far as I'm concerned there *is* no accommodation problem. Two people, two beds—what could be more logical?'

'Two cabanas!' Kerry retorted curtly, forgetting her resolution not to lose her temper. Then, on an impulse she couldn't rationalise, she added, 'I've no intention of becoming a substitute for Belinda Fraser!'

'I wasn't aware that I'd asked you to.' Merciless eyes

swept over her flushed face to travel with appreciative regard to her toes then back again to meet her outraged expression. 'Believe me, you couldn't substitute for Belinda if you tried!'

CHAPTER SEVEN

'BELIEVE me, I haven't the slightest intention of trying!' Kerry strode with quick steps towards the door. She'd asked for that laconic put-down, so why should it sting her pride so much? She might not have Belinda's wealth or beauty, but why should Mel be so certain she couldn't emulate some of her other qualities if she tried? Was she so lacking in social graces and intelligence?

'Hey, wait! Not so fast.' The wry amusement had left his face as he stepped round her, barring her exit. 'You seem to be showing a great deal of unwarranted interest in my love-life—or should I say lack of it?'

'Why not?' She contrived an air of insouciance. 'You've certainly shown enough interest in mine—let's just say I'm returning the compliment. Besides. . .' She couldn't help her mouth twitching with amusement as his stony gaze lingered on her face. 'To be honest with you, I find it rather amusing that you didn't get things all your own way for once. I'm sure Belinda's kicking over the traces provided you with a salutary lesson—that is,' she hastened to qualify, 'if the newspaper reports were factual.'

'Factual enough.' He stood, still barring her way, his expression unreadable. 'So you can rest assured I'm a free man again, free to go on sowing my wild oats, as the saying goes.'

'But not with me.' The words came out more gently than she'd intended, but she'd seen the glimmer of pain in his grey eyes. Not normally vicariously curious, she would have loved to have encouraged him to confide further in her. Whatever Belinda had meant to him, there was no doubt that the break-up of their relationship had hit him hard. An unexpected spasm of shame at her earlier outburst made her unable to hold his regard.

'Whatever you say, sweetheart.' The words conveyed indifference, but there was something in the deep tone of his reply, an intonation of knowing amusement that implied that, whatever it was she said, she wouldn't say it consistently. Before she could protest, he moved away, his hand rising to rub his chin. 'God! I need a shave. Give me fifteen minutes and I'll take you to dinner.'

She could have retorted she'd find her own way to the dining-room, but what was the point of alienating him? Whatever attitude he intended to take with her, she preferred him calm rather than aroused. An unfortunate choice of word. Her mind sheered away from its narrower implication, and to hide her confusion she asked quickly, 'Did you have a pleasant afternoon?'

'Yeah, great!' He was already in the bathroom, and she could hear the shower running. 'I went up to the sports centre and renewed some old friendships. Ended up having a game of golf, and finished the round on the seventh hole with some of the guys.' There was a short pause. 'They're all quite anxious to meet you, so I said we'll probably go along to the sports complex tomorrow and have a game of tennis.'

'I don't play.' It was an absolute lie, but he couldn't be allowed to have everything his own way, and she needed to practise saying no to him.

'No worries. We can go riding up at the farm instead, or I'll take you paragliding.'

His affability grated on her nerves. 'And suppose I said I didn't want to partake in all these strenuous activities?' she enquired acidly.

'I wouldn't believe you, Kerry.' The bathroom door was dragged open and he appeared on the threshold, a towel knotted firmly round his waist, half of his face covered in shaving-soap. 'Unless, of course, you persuaded me that you and Nick intended to spend all the time in bed. In which case I should have to seriously consider alternative plans.'

Kerry stared at him. Now she knew where she'd seen men with similar superb musculature, the broad shoulders, the flat, corrugated surface of abdomen, the trim waist. . .on the starting-blocks for the Olympic hundred metres breast-stroke final!

'All I want to persuade *you* of is that, despite all the evidence to the contrary, Nick Albioni and I have never been lovers, and neither was it my intention to alter the status quo; but it seems my hopes of doing that are zero,' she said coldly, then, deciding to change the subject, 'Is it really necessary for you to shave twice a day?'

'Only when I'm going to spend the night with a lady.' He'd returned to the bathroom and his voice drifted out to her, accompanied by the sound of much splashing. 'It's one of the hallmarks of a gentleman—that and taking one's weight on one's elbows—or so I've always been told. Shan't keep you much longer now. You'd better turn your back if you're going to be affronted by my putting my pants on.'

Kerry turned her back, hearing the rasp of a zip, and trying to keep her temper. It was difficult to say which infuriated her the most. Mel McKinley laying down the law, or Mel McKinley putting on a show of good-humoured companionship laced with doubtful innuendo. If he'd been consistent it would have been easier to formulate a plan to combat him. As it was, he kept dodging beneath her guard. . .

'OK, we can go now.'

In close-fitting cream trousers and a casual dark brown sports shirt he looked like a man any girl would readily accept as an escort—unless she knew what a pig-headed bore he could be!

Offered a drink at the bar, Kerry chose a pina colada, feeling a desperate need for something cool and easy to drink. It was delicious, but she refused a second one.

There was bound to be wine with dinner, and she needed to keep a clear head. When one of Mel's friends from the sports centre came up and slapped him on the back, she found herself introduced as his girlfriend. She accepted the description with a tight little smile, waiting till he'd gone before voicing her annoyance.

'Suppose if I told him the truth? That you were the director of the company I work for, and I'm not emotionally involved with you at all?'

Mel sighed. 'Sweetheart, it's for your sake. I'm afraid if I told them that, it would be nudge, nudge, wink, wink, every time we met, and you might not appreciate the laid-back type of Aussie humour you'd encounter.'

A cold anger brought a shiver to Kerry's bare neck and arms as she slid off the high bar-stool. 'If you told them the *whole* truth—that I don't want to share a holiday with you, let alone a cabana, and that far from caring for me you're twisted enough to try and mete out some sort of punishment for sins which you consider mortal and which I've never committed—then I'd hope that they'd punch you on your newly shaven jaw—and hard!' She spoke softly and swiftly, her eyes bright with pain and the sheer frustration of her position.

'Not here. Not now.' He was standing beside her, placing an arm round her shoulders, no sign of humour on his face, just a tight-drawn look, whether of anger or regret she couldn't tell. 'I don't fight in public, besides, you'll feel differently about it when you've had dinner.'

She wouldn't; but she allowed him to lead her to the *maître d'*, and was relieved to find that she and Mel would be sharing a large round table with three other couples. At least she wouldn't have to search for conversation when all she felt like was tipping her soup over his handsome head.

Two hours later she felt decidedly more mellow, good food, wine and company having wrought its customary magic. The other couples were all Australian, and had plied her with questions about London as well as sharing, at her request, their experiences in towns as far apart as Adelaide and Brisbane.

'Ready for bed yet, or would you like a nightcap at the bar?' Mel asked politely as they emerged into the spacious lounge. 'I think there's going to be dancing later tonight.'

'A drink would be nice.' Given such a choice it was the only possible answer. A sudden thought struck her. If she could persuade Mel to take a steady intake of alcohol, he might very well go to sleep as soon as his head touched the pillow. She'd prefer him to be disarmed when she carried out the transfer of the chairs, and alcohol might just be the answer. Of course, *she* would have to stay quite sober. That way she would have the upper hand. Momentarily she regretted the pina colada and the two glasses of wine she'd already imbibed, but the night was young.

'What'll it be, then? Another pina colada?' he asked solicitously.

'No, I. . .' Desperately her mind sought for something long and cool and totally non-alcoholic. Inspiration came in a flash, as she recalled two young children beside the pool earlier that morning. She'd have what they'd been drinking.

'Could I have a milkshake?' she asked, smiling winningly, her heart dancing a habanera in her chest in case he insisted she had something stronger. She knew from experience how some men would react. Hopefully, Mel McKinley, for all his sins, wouldn't be so gauche as to query her order.

'Right! One Dunk Island milkshake coming up.' Only his raised eyebrows suggested surprise at her choice.

Settling herself comfortably in one of the large armchairs by a glass-topped table, Kerry watched him make his leisurely way to the bar. Dinner had been a marvellous experience. She thought with pleasure of the

delicious oyster soup followed by succulent lamb cutlets
with all the trimmings, and the traditional Australian
pavlova—a different confection entirely from the type
produced in the UK. If all the food was as good as this
she would have to watch her waistline.

'Can we join you?' It was one of the couples with
whom they'd dined.

'Please do!' Gratefully Kerry seized on the opportunity
of company. 'Mel's just getting me a drink.'

'He's a right beaut guy, isn't he?' Kylie Thomas, a
large, blonde, middle-aged Brisbane housewife commented as her husband threaded his own way to the bar.
'*They* don't come ten for a dollar, more's the pity.'

Kerry stretched her mouth into an answering smile,
and nodded. This was neither the place nor the time to
express her own opinion.

Two and a half hours and four milkshakes later she
was dancing with the same real beaut guy, held close in
his arms, her red-gold head nodding against his shoulder
as he tightened his grasp round her waist. The band had
exhausted their repertoire of pop, and had resorted to
soft mood music, the lights were dim, and she felt
decidedly woozy.

Tiredness and anxiety, she thought, as she allowed
Mel's firm thighs to guide her round the small dancing
area. Not that this was real dancing, more like making
love to music. The thought should have appalled her.
Instead she wanted to giggle. Of course she should have
refused to dance with him when he'd asked her, only
strangely she couldn't remember his asking her. One
moment she'd been sitting nodding wisely as Kylie had
related her horror on turning up one of her old dining
chairs and finding a nest of red-back spiders beneath the
seat, and the next she'd been on the dance-floor.

'Happy, sweetheart?' His voice was a soft breath in
her ear, his hand a steady pressure on her lower back.
He smelled delicious. More delicious than the oyster

soup—but different, of course. Could it be the shaving-soap? Kerry lifted her head and tried to sniff at his lean cheek. He moved slightly and her lips made contact with his smooth skin. It wasn't what she'd intended, but it was an interesting experience. Tentatively she tested his cheek with the tip of her tongue. Yes, definitely smooth. He'd been quite right to shave.

'Kerry. . .' It was half impatience, half irritation, half something else. No, that didn't make sense. You couldn't have three halves. Damn it, she was more tired than she'd thought possible. That walk in the rainforest must have taken more out of her than she'd thought possible. If she felt like this on milkshakes, heaven knew what Mel felt like. Thank heavens she hadn't allowed him to talk her into altering her drink, although the fourth time she'd asked for a repeat order he'd suggested she tried something different. Fortunately, she thought smugly, she'd quelled that suggestion with polite insistence! She wasn't certain what Mel himself had been imbibing since dinner, but it had definitely been alcoholic, and he hadn't been a sluggard in going back to the bar.

She sighed deeply. 'Mel. . .?'

'Yes, sweetheart?' His reply was a soft, trembling murmur in his firm throat.

'I want to tell you something.'

She felt his body change, become tense, expectant. 'Tell me, Kerry.'

'It's a very good job that you're not driving tonight.'

There was a silence while he continued to guide her gently to the soft, smoochy beat, and she wondered if she should repeat her observation—if he hadn't heard her. Then she heard him sigh, felt the shudder of regret that robbed his body of tension, without understanding its source.

'As a matter of fact,' he said gently, 'it doesn't appear as if I'm going to do anything much tonight except sleep.

That is,' he added thoughtfully, 'unless your snoring keeps me awake.'

'I don't snore!' Outraged, Kerry managed to lift her head far enough away to meet his amused gaze.

'Oddly enough, I never really thought you did,' he told her inexplicably and, while her brow wrinkled trying to make sense of his quick contradiction, he stopped dancing, put a firm arm round her waist and said quietly but adamantly, 'Time for bed, sweetheart.'

Kerry stretched luxuriously, turning her head on the comfortable pillow. Did she smell coffee? Still only half awake, she opened her eyes and immediately the events of the previous day flooded back to her. Hastily she sat upright, relieved, yet at the same time dismayed, to discover she was still wearing her turquoise dress. Through the gap in the curtains she could see the sun slanting through the trees, as consternation surged like a tidal wave through her being. Despite all her good resolutions, she had spent the night in the cabana!

What had happened? She could recall events clearly up until the time Mel had escorted her back to the cabana. It was then that they became a little confused. To her chagrin she couldn't remember putting up any resistance when he'd guided her to one of the beds and suggested she let sleep claim her, it having seemed perfectly natural to curl up at his command. She even remembered having difficulty in undoing the tiny buckle of her sandals before lifting her legs on to the bed, but presumably she'd coped because her feet were bare.

She must have been extraordinarily tired, because she'd even gone to bed without taking off her make-up, she recollected. More to the point, where was her unwelcome room-mate, and where had he spent the night?

An unwilling glance at the bed separated by a small table from her own provided the grim answer to the second part of the question. The pillow still bore the shape of a human head, the dishevelled covers suggested the recent emergence of a body.

As if to confirm her findings, Mel emerged from the bathroom, dressed in a pair of violently coloured Bermudas.

'How do you want your coffee, sweetheart? Black?'

She would have liked to have refused any favour from him, but her mouth was incredibly dry, and there was no point in ineffective martyrdom.

'Black will be fine, thank you,' she answered primly.

'How's the head?' he enquired solicitously, placing the cup and saucer on the table beside her and smiling down in her direction.

'Fine!' She turned surprised hazel eyes in his direction. 'Why shouldn't it be? I was just tired last night, not drunk!'

'Of course you weren't drunk,' he mollified her instantly. 'Just very relaxed and warm and wonderful.'

Kerry's hand shook as she lifted the cup to her lips. 'If you're trying to suggest that—that anything happened between us—then you're wasting your time. If you'd laid as much as a finger on me I would have known!'

'Peace, Kerry!' Mel lifted his hands in mock surrender. 'I've never taken advantage of a lady whose judgement was impaired by a slight over-indulgence in alcohol. On the other hand, I think I've proved my point that it's possible for us to share the same cabana without the end of the world occurring, don't you?'

'I appreciate your restraint.' Sarcasm gave her voice an edge. 'I admit it was more than I expected from you in view of your threats.'

'Perhaps even more than you deserved?' he suggested lightly. 'After your lack of discretion last night? Or were you pinning your faith in the old adage that a man can't make love to a woman who is drunk or has a broken leg?'

'I was *not* drunk!' she said tightly. 'I was only tired. It takes more than one pina colada and two glasses of white wine to affect my judgement.'

'Such as four Dunk Island milkshakes, or have you forgotten your predilection for them?' The laughter lurking behind his eyes irritated her.

'Frankly I find your teasing infantile,' she retorted sharply. 'I saw some children drinking them at the poolside, and if they're suitable for four-year-olds, I imagine my metabolism can cope.'

'Ah. . .' He sat down on his own bed, propping his elbow on his knee and leaning forward, hand clasped to chin. 'What exactly did you think you were drinking, Kerry?'

A terrible suspicion made her pulse beat faster. 'Why—milk, cream and coffee flavouring.'

'The coffee flavouring was Kahlua.'

'But that's a liqueur, isn't it?' She could feel anger winding a tight band round her chest.

'Uh-huh, so are Drambuie and Galliano, and I don't have to tell you what Scotch is. I regret to tell you your milkshake contained the lot.'

'You—you absolute swine!' She was off the bed, shaking with fury plus the unsteadiness her sudden movement had caused. 'Spiking a drink is the lowest form of sabotage one human being can inflict on another. It's totally unforgivable. I might have been very ill!'

Disappointment was a very real element of her feelings. Somehow she had thought Mel McKinley above that kind of unspeakable behaviour. Heat suffused her body as she remembered how she had felt, locked in his arms on the dance-floor.

'Hey—hey. . .' He rose to his feet, towering over her. 'Don't blame me, sweetheart; you ordered the drink and I confirmed it with you before ordering. You remember—A Dunk Island milkshake?'

'Yes, but. . .' She looked dumbly at him.

'It's the name of a cocktail. There were several lists on the bar; I thought you must have remembered it from when we had our pre-dinner drink.' His brow furrowed in disbelief. 'You mean to say you honestly didn't realise? You didn't taste the alcohol in it?'

'No. . .it was sharp and smooth and sweet, and tasted of coffee, but I wasn't really paying attention to it—I was too interested in what Kylie and the others were discussing. Besides, I've never had a milkshake before; I didn't know what to expect.' She saw the lines at the side of his eyes begin to crinkle, and burst out, 'Don't you dare laugh at me. It could have been disastrous! Why didn't you try and stop me?'

'From my point of view it *was* disastrous.' The corners of Mel's mouth turned down in a rueful grimace. 'I'd planned a pleasant walk by the water's edge in the moonlight before bringing you back here to discuss our sleeping habits in an informal and relaxed atmosphere, and you neatly thwarted all my designs by falling asleep on me.' He ignored her small cry of protest. 'And as for stopping you, I did try, Kerry, but you don't take advice too easily, do you? And I don't believe in brute force. Mind you, if I'd realised just what an innocent you were I would have put you wise immediately.'

'Truly?' she asked miserably, reluctantly recognising the honesty of his assertion.

'Truly,' he responded firmly. 'Luckily there's no harm done, and you don't even have a hangover.'

'My poor dress!' Ruefully she surveyed the creased and crumpled fabric. 'Talk about a rag!'

'Mmm,' he surveyed her thoughtfully. 'In the circumstances I thought it better not to help you undress. I guessed you might have felt a little humiliated to wake up wearing nothing but your underclothing—provided, that is, you were even wearing any, and it didn't seem quite the gentlemanly thing to take any action which would reveal the answer.'

'And you expect me to thank you for not molesting me?' The colour flared in Kerry's cheeks as she realised the full extent of her helplessness the previous evening. Worse still there was a lurking memory of how right it had felt when he had placed her so gently on the bed. Her judgement had been sorely impaired, she had to admit, and if he had started to disrobe her, heaven knows how she would have reacted!

'No.' He answered her question after barely a moment's consideration. 'No, Kerry, my reward will come later.'

'What do you mean?' Even as the question left her lips she knew she was acting foolishly, encouraging him to exploit her weakness, like a poor tennis player madly chasing balls from a superior opponent round the court, leaving herself open to being smashed into oblivion at his pleasure.

'Mean?' His grey eyes were pools of innocence. 'Why, Kerry, I mean that when the times comes for me to undress you it will be with your consent and for our mutual pleasure—and *that* will be reward enough for my chivalry.'

He regarded her steadily, his eyes darkened with anticipation as she tried to find the words to refute his suggestion that she would ever agree to allowing such liberties.

'And now I'm going to put a shirt and shorts on and I'll be off to do some beachcombing. You'll have the whole cabana to yourself—all the privacy of a private room. I'll meet you in the dining-room in an hour's time for a champagne breakfast.'

'Champagne?' she shuddered, relieved at the change of subject.

'Best possible drink to put you back on top of the world. Then after breakfast I'll take you for a walk over the golf course and we can visit the farm, and I'll get you a real milkshake, fresh from the Jersey herd, so you'll be able to tell the difference.'

He was taking charge but, oddly, she didn't resent it. Perhaps she was still a little shaky after all those milkshakes, but it was strangely comforting to have Mel organising events on her behalf, and the programme he'd suggested sounded an ideal way of passing the time.

'Mel!' she burst out in despair. 'Tell me, did I do anything stupid last night? I think I can remember everything, but I'd like to know.'

'You want the truth?' He waited for her to nod. 'You were perfect, Kerry. I only wished the evening had lasted a little longer. Believe me, you have nothing whatsoever to be ashamed of.' He dipped his head and placed a chaste kiss on her forehead before she'd had time to realise his intention and draw away. 'Now let me get changed and we can start up from where we left off last night when you went to sleep on me.'

Touching her forehead where his lips had rested for such a brief moment, Kerry shivered, a brief, physical reaction to what she could only take as a threat. He had marked her as easy game, and after the break-up of his affair with Belinda he must be anxious to assert himself as a virile male animal, to soothe his wounded ego. . .and what better way than to avail himself of a woman whose ethics allowed her to romp around with a man whose wife had already borne him two children and was expecting the third?

'I thought you had already changed,' she called out, wrenching her mind away from images she preferred not to dwell on. 'Can't you wear Bermudas to breakfast?'

'Yeah—no worries. But strictly speaking these aren't for daylight wear. I usually sleep naked, but out of deference to having a cabana-mate I decided to add them to my wardrobe. Of course, I hadn't originally packed for a holiday, but I decided to leave my shopping until we reached Cairns. That's why I took the day off when you took the tour to the Great Barrier Reef. All in all I think I did quite well.'

He emerged wearing brief navy shorts and a soft cotton T-shirt, conservative but obviously expensive.

'Don't forget, Kerry. One hour and you'll be able to break your fast in style.'

In fact she was ready in half the time allotted, choosing to wear brief scarlet shorts and a white T-shirt, slipping her feet into casual flatties for the proposed walk.

When Mel returned from his stroll along the beach she was standing by the hibiscus pool, her face alight with pleasure, her mind temporarily distanced from the problem his presence posed her.

'I've just seen the most fabulous blue butterfly!' she cried out. 'Oh, Mel, it was exquisite, just like the one stencilled on the bottom of the pool. I've never seen anything like it before. It must have had a wing span of at least four inches, and the colour was incredible!'

'Papillio Ulysses joesa. . .' he murmured good-humouredly. 'The symbol of Dunk. First point to you, sweetheart. I've yet to see one this visit. They're pretty rare this time of the year, so consider yourself particularly favoured. Come on, we'd better make a start on breakfast; we've a long programme ahead of us!'

Nothing loath Kerry accompanied him to the dining-room. Why not make the most of her time on Dunk? If Mel became too obnoxious she could always walk away and leave him. She suppressed a sigh. The real dilemma was that his influence on her was subtle. He seemed to have the capacity to lull her into an unprotected calm and, just when she was beginning to enjoy his company, remind her of the low esteem in which he held her. Everything would have been a lot easier if she had been able to detest him as much as he despised her. But she had to be honest with herself. She might detest the attitude he'd taken towards her—but the man himself? No. Whatever she felt towards Mel McKinley she could not honestly say that she hated him. Neither had she any wish at that moment to analyse her emotions in an attempt to understand them.

Declining the champagne, she settled for pure orange juice followed by toast and marmalade and coffee, while Mel fed his virile male body with a full Australian breakfast, at a speed which suggested he must have felt close to starvation.

'Ready?' He crumpled his paper napkin on the table, eyeing her empty plate as he laid down his own knife and fork. 'Or do you want a second helping of toast?'

She shook her head, amazed at her own sense of expectation. Was it possible that, with a little give and take, the two of them could enjoy each other's company for a morning despite the unsettled issues which lay between them.

'Lead on, McKinley!'

CHAPTER EIGHT

THE only sounds to break the silence were the isolated calls of birds and the murmur of the cicadas as they took a leisurely meander past the tennis courts and the sports complex of the resort, to the small golf course.

'Not regretting you decided to stay?' Mel asked softly, as they approached the high-lying third hole.

Kerry shook her head, shading her eyes with her hands as she made out the outline of Mung-um-gnackum against the cloudless sky. 'Not yet. It's so special here that the price is almost worth the pain.'

'Of losing Albioni, do you mean? Or having to share your cabana with someone you detest?'

'No—I meant. . .' What had she meant? She wasn't quite sure herself. Certainly losing Mel McKinley's respect was a part of it, and she supposed the other part was the frustration of being unable to prove to him that she'd never been chasing after another woman's husband. There was no point in covering well-trodden ground. He had tried her on circumstantial evidence, and found her guilty. By any standards of justice his behaviour was absymal, so why should she feel the need to try and explain her feelings about him—particularly as she was none too certain of them herself? Perhaps it was because she had discerned an unusual note of bitterness in his deep voice.

She sighed. 'I don't detest you, Mel, only the arbitrary way in which you make judgements.'

'Someone has to.' There was nothing apologetic in his tone as he sank down on the grass. 'We might as well sit down and admire the scenery for a while.' He waited until she'd joined him on the ground, then added contemplatively, 'I'd like to believe you, sweetheart, especially after my restraint last night. Trouble is that you're such a terrible little liar.'

'I am not!' Her mood ruined, Kerry shot him a reproachful look. 'It's just that you can't see the truth when its glaring you right in the face.'

He regarded her affronted expression with some satisfaction, which only served to enrage her more. 'How come, then, I overheard you telling Kylie last night that you belonged to a tennis club in England, yet you told me you didn't play? I also remember your telling me that you snored. I know from experience now that that's a lie, too.'

'They were strategic lies!' Kerry defended herself sturdily, bemoaning the perversity which had goaded her into senseless antagonism.

'So is denying a relationship with Nick Albioni in the interests of keeping your job.' His tone was dry.

'There's no reasoning with you. . . You're determined to believe the worst of me!' She started to struggle to her feet, the whole mood of the morning dissipated, but Mel seized her arm and drew her down hard so that she fell towards him, her head landing with a dull thud on his midriff.

'Hush!' he commanded sternly, placing a firm hand across her waist to hold her in a steady position. 'As well as being sparing with the truth, you've got a terrible temper on you, Kerry Davies. I suppose it's because when you were a little girl you didn't have a father around to spank you when you threw a tantrum.'

'That's right. I didn't.' She had long come to terms with being fatherless, so there was no reason for the tears which threatened her, unless it was the choking feeling of frustration which seemed to assault her whenever she was in such close proximity to her grandfather's prickly partner. 'Perhaps I should count the absence of paternal chastisement as a blessing,' she retorted crisply. 'It's about the only one that springs to mind at the moment.'

'As a blessing it's not without value, sweetheart, believe me. It's not much fun being chased round the yard with a stock-whip, either.'

'You?' she asked in astonishment, flinching as she recalled the knotted leather whips which were used on the Australian stock farms. Just the crack of them set the nerves jangling. 'Are you saying your father took a whip to you?' She was so startled by the idea that she forgot her own indignation.

'My stepfather,' he said lazily. 'And only once—but it was enough.'

The hand round her waist loosened, but Kerry made no effort to move. Her head was so close to his heart that she could hear its deep, steady beat just as clearly as she had discerned the pain in his bald statement. Suddenly she wanted to know more—much more.

'But—but I thought Bob McKinley was your *father*,' she said at last, keeping her voice low so as not to break the strange spell that seemed to have settled over the two of them. She'd never expected confidences from her self-assured companion, but she could sense his need, and her tender heart went out to him.

'Yeah, Bob was my father, but he and my mother split up when I was three years old. Problem was that Dad spent all his time at work, building up McKinleys to become a viable business, when he wasn't getting my mother pregnant. It was the mid-fifties, and coach travel was just about taking off, but he needed to work twenty hours a day to make even a small profit.' He paused, and Kerry felt his hand move gently against her ribs. 'Thing was, my mother didn't understand. There she was with two daughters of seven and five, and me, just turned three. A beautiful woman with no social life and an absentee husband, so when she met a wealthy New

Zealand stockbreeder who was visiting Perth for the sailing, she upped and left, taking us kids with her.'

There was a short, strained silence while Kerry assimilated the scope of such a disruption on his young life, then, making an effort to inject lightness into her voice she said, 'So you were brought up in New Zealand?'

'Until I was sixteen, yes. Oh, it wasn't a bad life.' He plucked a blade of coarse grass and chewed at its tender end. 'Dad divorced my mother and she married my stepfather. Unfortunately the two of us never got on. He was fine with my sisters, but he never could stand the sight of me, although to do him justice he tried to hide the fact.'

'Perhaps you reminded him too much of your father? Of the man who had loved your mother before he did?' Kerry suggested gently.

'I guess there's some truth in that,' he agreed wearily. 'I certainly favoured him in looks. In retrospect I can see how my mother started to ignore me when he was around, probably so as not to increase his antagonism against me.' He gave a harsh laugh. 'At the time I just thought I was unlovable.'

'Oh, Mel. . .' Kerry could feel the hurt and incomprehension of the small boy, and wept inwardly for him.

'My tender-hearted Kerry!' This time his laugh held gentle amusement. 'On the other hand I wasn't the easiest teenager in the world. From about thirteen onwards we couldn't see each other without brawling, and my poor mother had to bear the brunt of our continual disagreements until the day I went too far and he came for me with the stock-whip.'

'Oh, God!' she breathed, her heart increasing its beat in sympathy with the fear he must have felt.

'It's OK, sweetheart, he didn't flay me alive, although at the time I was sure he meant to.' His eyes narrowed to slits, Mel focused on the cloudless sky above them. 'I think he just meant to scare the living daylights out of me. If so, he surely succeeded! As I took to my heels it was my pride that was stung rather than my flesh. I spent that night with a friend, went home the next day when he was out, borrowed some money from my mother, and left home for good.'

'What did you do then?' Fascinated by this revelation of his past, Kerry eased herself up, propping herself on one elbow to gaze down on his face.

'Got a passage to Sydney and hitch-hiked my way to Perth. It took longer than I'd expected, and I was dirty and hungry by the time I located my father.' He stretched, putting his hands behind his head and regarding Kerry through narrowed eyes. 'He'd never forgiven my mother, and he'd never got in touch with us children. I knew he'd be bitter, but at least he was my own flesh and blood. As I said, I even resembled him, which I thought might make him regard me more favourably.'

'And did it?'

Mel smiled, a slow, lazy twist of his hard mouth. 'As long as I live I shall never forget our first meeting. I walked into his office and said, "Mr McKinley, I'm your son." And he looked me up and down for about two minutes, then drawled, "So what?"'

'Oh, Mel!' Kerry's horror echoed in her voice. All this time she'd believed that Mel McKinley had been born with a silver spoon in his mouth—an only son destined through birth alone to be successful. It seemed she couldn't have been more wrong.

He grinned at her dismay. 'After that, things improved remarkably fast. He'd never remarried and he was secretly delighted to see me again, although he hid his pleasure with extreme toughness. He took me into the business at the bottom, gradually training me on until I got my driving licence. Then he made sure I drove on all the routes and learned all the problems from the driver's point of view. It was the way he worked himself, and one of the reasons for McKinleys' high standing in the business.'

'You were very fond of him, weren't you?' Kerry asked softly, aware of the gap in her own heart which could have held a father's love.

'Yup!' He pulled himself into an upright position. 'We worked together for twelve years. Then, in one freak accident two years ago while he was out sailing, it all ended. He was only fifty-nine—a man still in his prime.' He paused, while Kerry kept silent, watching the lines of pain etch themselves into his face as the muscles of his jaw tightened. 'And do you know the most damnable thing about it all was that I never told him how much I—I admired and respected him!'

He hadn't been able to say 'love', but that was clearly what he meant. Kerry sighed, a long-drawn-out exhalation of breath.

'He would have known, Mel,' she said at last firmly, her eyes bright with reassurance. 'It's not possible to hide deep feelings from someone close to you, especially if they care for you too.'

'Isn't it?' His mouth twisted into a rueful smile, as his light eyes dwelt with deadly seriousness on her eager face. 'Then you know how I feel about you?'

'Decidedly!' Glad that he'd decided to leave his sad memories, Kerry answered him with some tartness. 'You've made your opinion of me very clear from the first time we met.'

'Then I think the time's come to reinforce it.'

Before she had a moment to collect her thoughts, he reached for her, taking her by the shoulders, pulling her down on the grass beside him, holding her face between his hands and seeking her lips with his own. His response was so different from what she'd expected that she made no attempt to evade him, letting him possess her mouth, clasping his firm body against her own, smoothing his back with loving hands, calming and comforting the small boy who had mourned his father as she had mourned hers, loving the man he had become.

'My sweet, sweet Kerry!' The fingers of one hand laced through her hair, while the others found the warm swell of her breast, caressing it with urgent fingers through the light cotton covering. 'So fiery, yet so warm and giving. . .'

His mouth trembled against her cheek, nuzzled her neck, while she threw her head back, accepting his tributes, feeling her body blossom and surge with powerful forces.

Instinctively she reached for him, running her hands down his ribcage, sliding them beneath his loose shirt, shuddering with delight as she touched his warm, firm flesh and heard him utter a harsh, broken cry. He pulled her down on him, then, turning so that she was trapped beneath him, aware of every contour of his hard body, frightened yet excited by his very physical reaction to her proximity. It was a moment of pure magic, making her feel in communication with the vibrant power of creation which seemed to hold the island in its thrall.

'I want you, Kerry. . . I want you so much it's becoming unbearable. . . All those nights on the tour, imagining you alone in your little room—because you *were* alone, my sweet, I made sure of that. Last night was purgatory for me. . . I didn't even dare to kiss you on the cheek in case I couldn't stop. Oh, God. . .' He was breathing harshly, punctuating his words with little kisses, tasting her like a butterfly sipping nectar. 'Do you understand what I'm saying?'

Kerry's stomach muscles tensed as she looked into his strong, handsome face and felt the heady response of every tingling fibre in her body. There was no logic to what was happening between them, but its presence was undeniable.

'Yes. . .of course I understand. . .'

Was it only minutes ago that he had stirred up her

resentment? Or were those emotions false, a protective cover to cushion her own ego against what she'd seen as his contempt? Her life had contained its fair share of male friends and acquaintances, some she had liked, some not, but there'd never been anyone who could push her to the limits of her own emotions in the way Mel McKinley could.

His predatory gaze glinted over her, as he caressed her upper arms with sure fingers, inciting a shimmering fire to dance on her skin. Her confused mind envisaged the chaos those lean hands could wreak on the rest of her body. He could fascinate her, charm her, infuriate her, but above all disturb her, wrecking her usual sang-froid.

It was as if her whole world had turned upside-down and left her gasping. Mel McKinley was a dangerous brew, but she wanted to taste him, drain him to the dregs. For the first time in her life she experienced the wild tug of desire. Not the peaceful, contented sensation of happy companionship, but the jagged, searing excitement of being caught up in a maelstrom of feeling, tossed like a rudderless ship in a cyclone. She was shocked by its power—left gasping by the betrayal of her own hormones as they responded to his male dominance.

'Kerry, sweetheart.' He sensed her uncertainty and kissed her again, his mouth hard and sure, telling her without words that he wouldn't allow her to deny the reaction she had already given him. 'Admit you want me to love you. Say I'm not misreading the tension that's simmered between us ever since you burst unannounced into my office with your demands?'

'It wasn't a demand—it was a request. . .' she began indignantly, then, seeing the sparkle of his eyes, lapsed into silence.

'Sparks,' he said softly. 'We struck sparks off each other and now we're caught up in the resulting blaze.' He kissed her once more, and she responded eagerly, moaning deep in her throat as the kiss deepened, his mouth avaricious as he claimed her with an arrogant sense of purpose. 'God knows, this wasn't what I intended when I decided to drive the tour myself,' he muttered. 'But day by day you've got under my skin until you've taken possession of all of my senses. You can't deny you want me as much as I want you,' he breathed against her cheek. 'Not when I can feel you blossom beneath my touch.' His voice thickened. 'Did Albioni make you feel like this? Did he, Kerry?'

She was being carried away on a springtide of dangerous emotion, aroused by his nearness and his husky declarations, and somehow she had to release herself from his power, from the persuasive influence of his hands and mouth, or she would be lost.

In the end it was easy. All she had to do was remind herself of just how low his opinion of her was, how he was using her as a substitute for the beautiful and unattainable Belinda, how it was her availability, not her desirability, which made her such an easy target.

'That's enough!' She forced her way out of his embrace, smoothing down her clothes as his expression hardened in disbelief. 'I may have been compelled to share a cabana with you, but that's as far as it goes! I hate being mauled! If you can't even respect me during the day——'

'Respect, Kerry?' His face had become stony, the grey eyes narrowed and evaluating. 'That's something which has to be earned, and to date I've seen very little evidence that you deserve it.'

'Why you——' Biting back the angry epithet which sprang to her lips, Kerry tried to scramble upright, but a strong hand fastened around her arm, pinning her on the ground.

'Not this time, sweetheart.' Mel leaned over her, his face flushed, his eyes sharp, accusing points. 'This time it's my turn to point out a few home-truths. Murray thinks the world of you, and he's going to be pretty done up if he finds out that you've been playing fast and loose with a married man. In a way I feel sorry for Albioni— if you led him on the way you've led me on just now, he didn't stand a chance!'

'"The woman tempted me!" you mean?' Furiously she squirmed in his grasp. 'I suppose you mean to make it your business to repeat Nick's lies to my grandfather? Well, I promise you he won't believe them. He knows me better than that.'

'Does he? I wonder.' Mel surveyed her flushed face thoughtfully. 'But, no, you're quite wrong. I wouldn't want to disillusion him. Your grandfather is quite a guy. Losing his son when he did was a powerful blow. It's no wonder that he's pinned all his hopes for the future on you.'

'And I don't intend to let him down,' Kerry declared firmly. 'And that means not forming intimate relationships with casual acquaintances—particularly ones who allow their lust to overrule their conscience!'

'What a Puritan concept from a Chaucerian heroine!' Grey eyes glinted with the light of battle as he baited her. 'But you're forgetting one thing, sweetheart——' his mouth widened into a slow smile '—and that is that Murray has been trying to get the two of us together from the moment you arrived in Melbourne.'

Remembering the masquerade of her grandfather's birthday party, Kerry couldn't deny it. 'He's an elderly man. He has his aberrations,' she acknowledged unhappily.

'Aberrations, nothing! He wants to see his great-grandchild on the board of McKinleys,' Mel told her softly.

'An old man's fantasy,' she dismissed, but her heart increased its rhythm at the sudden image which flooded the screen of her mind.

'Perhaps.' The dark, gold-flecked head dipped slightly. 'But not one that you share?'

Kerry managed to shrug her shoulders. 'Hardly, since Murray's daydreams would include a wedding-ring before conception.'

'Ah!' Mel scrutinised her flushed face, a frown drawing his straight brows together across the bridge of his cleanly chiselled nose. 'So that's your price now, is it?'

Kerry met his gaze without flinching. He was being deliberately insufferable, taking pleasure from her attempts to justify herself. Well, at least she'd contest the point.

'Why not?' she said pleasantly. 'That way I shan't be deceived again by a man who is already married but prefers to keep the fact a secret.'

'So supposing I asked you to marry me?' he countered instantly. 'I'm a much better proposition than your Italian friend. More money, more influence, more status. . . Would you suddenly find my bed more attractive?'

Something like pain lanced through her—a feeling of sharp despair and loss, as unexpected as it was inexplicable. In that instant the taste of his mouth on hers, the scent of his skin, the warmth of his very male presence returned to taunt her.

'On the rebound?' she asked delicately, deciding to play him at his own game. 'I've never fancied an understudy's part. All the work, all the pain, and at the end of it all it's the star who gets the bouquets and the plaudits.'

'Not if she's left the production.'

He was much too close to her again. She could feel his soft breath on her cheek, sense the tension which held his strong body in thrall, knew that in the quaint little fencing match in which they were indulging it would be he, Mel, who would deliver the final most painful thrust. She should get to her feet, take to her heels, running across the deserted golf course until she was exhausted— but alone and safe.

'Forget about Belinda.' Kerry hadn't acted quickly enough, and now it was too late, as his hand rose to touch her cheek with a light caress. 'I told you—it's history. Ashes.'

'I'm sorry,' she whispered, shocked by the bleakness of his expression. 'Broken relationships are always painful.' She spoke the platitude not from any personal knowledge, but from an innate sense of compassion.

'Yeah.' He stared down at her, and she could see the thickness of his dark eyelashes, the specks of turquoise light which danced in the greyness of his sombre eyes. 'It must be tough for you too, Kerry. It can't be easy for you to be here alone when you'd been looking foward to sharing the time with someone you cared for.'

'It isn't.' She looked away, too full of mixed emotions to continue meeting his gaze. She *had* looked forward to sharing her time with Nick. But only her time—not her bed. Angrily she brushed a tear away, incensed by her own stupidity, and even more by the certain knowledge that through her naïveté she had forfeited the friendship of a man who had entered her life and turned it inside out.

'Then isn't there a chance that we can console each other after all, hmm?' His forefinger brushed her parted lips, and for a breathtaking moment Kerry thought he would follow the caress with his mouth.

Conscious that the strong drive of his virile body was in top gear, and overcome by panic and the realisation against all logic that she wanted desperately to give him the reassurance he demanded, she stared back at him, trying to form the words that would reject him once and for all, because to do anything else was to court disaster.

Before she could utter a sound there was a low rumbling guffaw from where the green gave way to rainforest.

'Oh, someone's watching us!' Embarrassment and relief filled her in equal measure as the spell was broken.

'Relax. It's only a kookaburra.' Mel sat up, controlling his breathing with an effort as she started to her feet.

'Is it?' she asked, still disbelieving and discomfited. 'It didn't sound like one to me.'

Mel gave a sigh of resignation. 'He always sounds dejected because he's the only one of his species on the island. Doomed to die unmated. That's why his laughter is hollow.'

'You're teasing me again.' Kerry was fast regaining her composure as she brushed strands of grass off her bare legs, grateful that the tension between them had snapped.

'No, I swear it's true.' He regarded her steadfastly. 'Seems he got blown off course and now he's paying the penalty for not being more careful.'

'Poor bird.'

Was Mel preaching at her again? It was difficult to tell, and she mustn't be over-sensitive or the rest of the holiday would be a disaster. The rest of the holiday! Would it really be possible for the two of them to go on sharing a cabana with this undercurrent of animosity and sexual chemistry never far from the surface? Mel's suggestion was ridiculous, of course. She wasn't broken-hearted about Nick, just hurt and angry, and the last complication she sought was the kind of consolation Mel was offering her. So why had it been so difficult to turn him down?

'That's life.' Mel shrugged philosophically. 'Some you win, some you don't. Come on, let's cool down our overheated blood with a ninety-nine-per-cent-pure Jersey milkshake!'

'Ninety-nine per cent?' Kerry queried doubtfully, relief flooding through her that he was calling an end to the brief episode of violent chemistry which had bubbled between them. 'What's the missing one per cent—vodka?'

'Strawberry flavouring, sweetheart!' he reassured her,

sweeping his gaze over her slim figure before lifting his eyes and allowing them to linger on her slightly parted lips. 'And while you're drinking it you can think about what I asked you.'

Consolation! Had Mel's feelings for Belinda been so shallow that he could heal the pain of their break-up by taking another woman to his bed? Kerry took a long swallow of the cold, creamy milkshake. Never again would she confuse the real thing with the exotic concoction she'd enjoyed with so much abandon the previous evening. Strange how Mel had accepted her ignorance of its potency, but still refused to accept that she had been equally duped by Nick Albioni's devious plan. Perhaps it was because he couldn't believe any girl could be so stupid, or perhaps since he had lost Belinda his opinion of womankind as a whole had become jaded.

She could understand his frustration—the blow his pride must have sustained—but to try and assuage it by using her as a substitute was humiliating. It reduced her to the level of a restorative for his ego—and yet. . . Mentally she could reject him, but physically her body ached to be close to him. After what had just happened between them she couldn't deny it. There was no sense to it. That was what troubled her most. For the first time in her life she was no longer in total control of her responses. Somewhere inside her brain was this small, insistent voice demanding to know if it would really be so impossible to snatch at the consolation she was being offered. Consolation not for Nick's absence, because as every hour passed she was thanking her lucky stars that she'd been saved the degradation of being compromised by him. Every minute the pink glow was clearing from the rose-tinted spectacles through which she had regarded him.

No, the solace she sought was for having been so sure of her own good judgement, when all the time she had had the brains of a stupid galah, as Murray would have said! She felt a cold shiver tease her spine. How humiliated she would have felt when the truth finally emerged, for common sense told her that Nick's married state couldn't have remained a secret forever—in fact, other employees of McKinleys were probably already aware of it! Grimly she admitted that she had Mel to thank for sparing her that scandal—even if his action hadn't been intended to be altruistic!

Handing back the now empty copper goblet, she wondered what Murray would be doing at that moment. Probably rubbing his hands together, convinced that Mel would be falling a victim of the beauty her grandfather insisted she possessed. It was just as well for the older man's peace of mind that he had no idea of the image Mel McKinley had of her, or of the dishonourable bent of his intentions!

'Ready?' Mel's voice broke into her reverie. Calm and matter-of-fact, it could have been the question of a mere acquaintance.

'Surely.' She followed his lead, smiling brightly as if the incident on the golf course had never occurred. But was she? Agonisingly aware of the confused feelings Mel had generated inside her from their first encounter, the way they had increased over their enforced closeness during the tour and her inability either to understand or control them, she was as far from ready to deal effectively with Mel McKinley as she had ever been!

CHAPTER NINE

'WE'LL come here for a gallop one morning.'

Mel had followed the passage of Kerry's eyes, and seen the surge of longing that had dilated the pupils, as he led her down past the deserted runway to the long sweep of Pallon Beach. Here, unlike the sheltered Brammo Bay, the sea had a more vigorous movement, evidence of driftwood and long bands of seaweed a tribute to its agitation, while tree-trunks bleached by the sun and salt-spray stood at angles as if pushed by some giant hand. Here there were no shady coconut palms, but rainforest trees and mangroves with their long, twisted, exposed roots perched precariously in the soft sand, which bore the unmistakable prints of horses' hoofs.

'I don't ride,' she told him sadly, as her imagination pictured her on a galloping steed, hair flying, while the breeze stung her cheeks and the Coral Sea flowed between its hoofs.

'Like you don't play tennis?' he taunted her.

'No, truly.' She accepted his scepticism as deserved. 'It's not the sort of hobby you take up when you're the child of a one-parent family.'

'I guess not.' The sudden seriousness in his voice was unexpected as he put an arm round her waist. She tensed at the intrusion into her body space so soon after the earlier flare of sensuality on the golf course, but lacked the resolve to move away. 'Was it bad for you, being brought up without a father?'

Touched by his interest, Kerry turned wide eyes to his intent face. 'Oh, no! I think it was a case of not missing what I'd never had, and Mother and I were very close. It's just that there wasn't a lot of money to spare for extras, but we never went without essentials.'

She walked a few paces in silence, remembering her childhood, accepting the firm touch of Mel's hand at her waist. 'Mum was the one who suffered. I remember hearing her weeping at night in the next room, and she always kept Dad's photograph on her bedside table.'

It was the first time she had ever told anyone about the trauma of growing up, trying to be both husband and daughter to the woman who had borne her. She didn't even stop to question why she was telling Mel. It just felt right.

'Poor Mum, she was the kind of woman who is so despised today.' She gave a bitter little laugh. 'She really needed a man to run her life. Not that she was stupid and clingy—just, well, just vulnerable, I guess you'd describe it. As I grew up I got used to taking charge, being responsible for the bills being paid on time, buying the tickets when we went out anywhere, taking the initiative. . .'

She paused, then sighed. 'She came to depend on me so much that I could never have left her for any length of time by herself. I'd longed so much to come here, to trace my grandfather, but Mum wouldn't hear of it—and then a miracle happened. She met Jack Wentworth, and fell in love for the second time in her life. . .and married him.'

'And you were free at last to fly, poor little butterfly?' Mel's fingers tightened on her slender waist, his voice vibrant with comprehension. 'And fly you shall, sweetheart. Before you leave Dunk I guarantee you'll soar into the heavens; and you shan't be deprived of the joy of an early-morning ride, either, although we'll restrict you to a walk rather than a gallop. They're used to beginners at the riding stables. I promise you, you'll come to no harm.'

Not from the ride perhaps, Kerry allowed silently, but

afterwards? The potent threat of his presence endangered the delicate equilibrium of her emotions. Her mind skittering away from attempting to analyse her reactions, she contented herself with a nod of acceptance.

Walking in a companionable silence, they crossed the sandspit at the west of the island, turning eastward into Brammo Bay, and continued until they returned to the Beachcomber resort.

Her emotions still churning, she had little appetite for lunch, and was happy with just a few king-size prawns and a small salad. Perhaps she should tell Mel now that she had no intentions of seeking consolation with him? On the other hand, he hadn't suggested a time limit, so why not enjoy the rest of the day? If he was as calculating as his previous behaviour had suggested, he would be on his best behaviour at least until sunset, wouldn't he?

If he broached the subject again she would be adamant and distant. Freeze him with the 'tight little accent' which seemed to amuse him so much. Yes, she would make one more determined effort to get her message across. And if that failed? Metaphorically she shrugged her shoulders. That was a problem she would deal with if and when it occurred. Surely an opportunist like Mel would stop banging his head against a brick wall and look elsewhere for the comfort he was seeking when he realised she meant what she said? Despite the warmth of the afternoon, Kerry shivered. There was one major problem. Before she would be able to convince Mel McKinley that she didn't want him as a lover, she would have to convince herself!

'Have you planned anything for this afternoon?' she asked, putting her knife and fork together on the plate, determined to force her mind away from her problems while the sun continued to shine.

'Uh-huh.' He slanted her an oblique look. 'I mean to give you a memorable day. You know, sweetheart, I could almost believe you enjoy someone else making the decisions on your behalf.' He raised a lazy eyebrow, inviting her to disagree.

'Sometimes,' she said guardedly. 'Particularly when their experience of the situation is greater than mine.' She saw the sudden glitter in his grey eyes, and added hurriedly, before he could speak, 'And you're no stranger to Dunk.'

He nodded. 'Even a place like this has its traumas, you know. A few years ago it took a mighty blow from a cyclone. Fortunately, there was hardly any structural damage to the resort buildings, but the canopy of foliage was ripped off and many of the trees came crashing down.' He made a grimace of pity. 'From the pictures I saw she looked like a collaborator shorn of her beauty, naked and torn.'

'But you'd never guess. . .' Amazed, Kerry looked at the verdant beauty surrounding her.

'Nature has a way of cleansing herself. It may have seemed cruel to us, but by routing out all the dead wood she left space for the new trees to grow, and by stripping off the canopy she made sure they had light and water, and, of course, the trees left standing recovered in time.'

Kerry shuddered. 'It seems so cruel.'

'Not really.' His mouth twisted into a wry smile. 'It's like the legend of the Phoenix—regeneration through destruction. Like life.' It was as if he was looking inward towards his own soul, repeating a hard-earned lesson.

I love him! The thought imprinted itself on Kerry's brain before she could shield it from the knowledge. Aghast at the insight into her own psyche, she felt her face drain of colour. No wonder she had been vacillating so much in her actions! It wasn't anything she could explain logically, and it added a terrifying dimension to her predicament!

'Kerry. . .' He had tuned into her distress as if he had felt the sharp edge of pain which had accompanied her comprehension of her own weakness. His hand reached across the table, covering her own. Unbearably sensitised, she flinched beneath its warmth. 'It will pass, believe me. The agony won't be sustained. He was never worthy of your love, and one day you'll realise that! There'll be someone else. Someone who is free to give you all the things you want.'

'No. . .' Her throat was so dry she had to take a sip of the tonic water she'd chosen to accompany her meal. 'You don't understand. . .'

'What it's like to see your dreams for the future exposed for what they are—built on shifting sands?' He laughed bitterly. 'You misjudge me, Kerry. It's far easier to build up a company from nothing than it is to achieve a relationship which will stand the test of time!'

Was he talking of his father's experience or his own? His expression was shuttered, the thick swathe of lashes masking the grey eyes which might have betrayed him. Kerry ached with a sudden longing to know what had happened between him and Belinda. Was it really as dead as he had insinuated? But reticence stilled her tongue as he lifted his hand from hers.

'But enough philosophising.' Pushing his chair away from the table, he offered her the assistance of his broad palm. 'I promised you you'd fly, and that's exactly what you're going to do!'

An hour later, buckled into a life-jacket and wearing a disreputable pair of rubber shorts over her trim, one-piece swimsuit, Kerry found herself strapped into the harness of a parachute—fulfilling his pledge!

Apprehensive, but determined not to let Mel suspect her qualms, she took the three running steps necessary, and found herself lifted smoothly into the air behind a fast speed-boat. The sensation was incredible. Joyously she gave herself up to the thrill of travelling through the air, gaining confidence by the moment, even taking one of her hands off the guide-line to wave to the man standing on the sandspit, head thrust back, watching

her. The man who against all probability had stormed
her heart.

How had it happened? Way beneath her the speed-
boat looked like a toy, its white wake painted on a sea of
almost hallucinatory beauty, as she tried to analyse her
feelings. It had started with reluctant admiration, she
realised, as she'd come to acknowledge Mel's capabilities, his patience and his dependability over the preced-
ing days.

Compared with Nick he was a giant—not just in
stature, she smiled to herself, but in character too. She
would never have desired him for his looks alone,
compelling though they were. It was the essential man
within that lean, beautiful male body she lusted after—
the soul of Mel McKinley. Earlier that day on the golf
course he had allowed her a glimpse of it, and she had
longed for a deeper insight. That was the moment the
self-deceiving veils had been dislodged from her eyes,
preparatory to the final revelation.

The boat slowed and she drifted downwards towards
the cyan sea. Lower and lower until her feet tipped the
surface, then her legs were submerged up to the knees
and she was treading water at speed like a dolphin before
rising swiftly to greater heights. It was over too soon, the
boat turning and making for the sandspit, manoeuvring
with great skill so that she landed both feet on firm
ground, to be gathered into Mel's arms as he saved her
from stumbling.

'I shall never forget this day as long as I live!' she told
him breathlessly as he helped her out of the harness and
the other protective clothing, hugging to herself the
revelation which would have to remain her secret.

'That's something I mean to make very sure of,' he
said very softly, brushing her lips with the whisper of a
kiss, inciting her whole body to shiver with apprehension. . . Surely a man of his experience would recognise
the signs of her newly perceived vulnerability? 'I mean

you to savour every sun-filled moment,' he continued softly. 'We can go for a swim now by the jetty where the water's still deep, then we can lie on the beach under the coconut palms, and if you're good I'll show you how to de-husk a coconut, so that you'll never starve to death if you're shipwrecked on a desert island.'

'You make everything sound so wonderful!' Breathlessly, Kerry slid an arm around his bare waist above the dark bathing-shorts which girded his lean loins, as they walked along the water's edge, indulging a wild urge to touch him, knowing she was playing with fire, and exhilarated when she heard the satisfaction in his soft laugh.

'And it's going to get more and more wonderful, sweetheart,' he promised. 'When we've had our fill of the beach we'll go back to the cabana to get ready for dinner. We won't be eating in the main restaurant tonight, because I've booked a table especially for us at Banfield's restaurant in the sports complex, where the menu is à la carte and very special indeed. And when that element of our appetites is replete, I shall take you down to the beach and we'll walk along the water's edge, and the moon will be full and bright and the palms will glow emerald-green in the garden spotlights.'

He paused, as Kerry felt her body shiver in a delicious anticipation. 'And,' he said huskily, 'all that time, I shall be thinking of the coming night, imagining sliding your clothes away from your lovely body, touching your fine skin with my hands and my mouth. . .running my fingers through your hair, and holding you so close to me that neither of us shall know where one ends and the other begins. . .because it's something we both want. Has been even before we set foot here. . .'

'Mel. . .no. . .' It was a half-hearted protest as Kerry felt an inner fire begin to build inside her, but he ignored the interruption.

'And,' he went on inexorably, 'all the time we're

having a normal civilised conversation, you'll know what I'm thinking—or at least a small part of it—and then it will be time to go back to the cabana together.'

Kerry swallowed with difficulty, her mouth abnormally dry. 'That's not what I want, Mel.' Even to her own ears the statement sounded untrue.

'No?' He looked at her, eyes narrowed against the glare of the sun. 'Why, Kerry? No ties—no commitments. Just the way you like it and, at the end of it, no broken hearts, no weeping wives, no regrets.'

'I need more time!' It was the wrong answer. Kerry knew it before the last word had left her lips. She had implied uncertainty. She should have said no, and repeated it until he had accepted her answer as final, because if she would have been hurt by becoming his lover when she hadn't even been aware of her feelings for him, how much more would she suffer loving him and knowing that to him she was as unimportant as any willing female?

'I'm a patient man.' The curl of his mouth belied the statement which, in any case, she knew to be false. Anyone less patient than Mel McKinley she had yet to meet! If she was wavering now, how much worse the decision she would face after an intimate dinner. . .

'Oh!' Dismay clouded her exclamation at the same time as she saw a road to escape. 'I haven't got anything to wear to dinner. I only packed two dresses because of the luggage limitation, and I haven't had time to get them laundered.'

'That problem, too, can be solved, Cinderella! Trust me!' It was as if he had anticipated her reluctance, and had contingency plans laid to override any emergency she might fabricate.

But before she could ask further questions he broke away from her, plunging into the sea to swim in a fast crawl towards the horizon.

Trust him! To do what? Pleasure her and leave her?

Because that was what the cards read unless she could rediscover the inner strength which had sustained her until now. The trouble was, of course, she had never been in love before.

Following Mel into the water, using a more leisurely stroke and keeping closer to the shore, her expression was bemused as the seeds he had planted in her mind began to grow.

It was early evening when they returned to the cabana and Mel claimed first use of the bathroom.

'I'll get shaved and showered and out of your way,' he said cheerfully. 'Then you can take your time and meet me in the Beachcomber Bar when you're ready, and we'll have a quick aperitif before going to Banfield's.'

Thankful that his manner was entirely void of any of the sensuality he had portrayed on the beach earlier, Kerry couldn't help but wonder if his change of attitude was part of a master plan to get his own way. He was an arch manipulator where business was concerned. Why shouldn't he display the same qualities where his personal life was concerned? She shook herself mentally. She must be going mad if she really thought he would put so much concentrated planning into seducing her. It wasn't as if he cared for her, was it? Quite the opposite, in fact. Probably it was all one big game with him and he was enjoying seeing her squirm! 'Tight little vowels', indeed!

'About my dress. . .' she began hesitantly, forcing her mind back to present problems. 'I suppose I could iron it. . .'

'No way.' His tone dismissed argument. 'We'll get it properly laundered tomorrow. For tonight, just leave everything to me.'

His tone brooked no argument, and she shut her mouth tightly. There was no need to thwart him unnecessarily. She sighed to herself. How was it possible to love someone so much it brought an ache to one's chest, and at the same time be so infuriated with everything about him that you wanted to fight him with any weapon, verbal or physical, that came to hand? All her life she had loved and protected her mother. Now, ironically, when she longed to confide the turmoil of her emotions to Louise, the older woman was thousands of miles away.

She was in the bathroom three-quarters of an hour later, showered and dressed in cotton briefs and bra, when she heard Mel's voice outside the door.

'I've solved your dress problem for tonight,' he told her. 'Come out and see what you think.'

'How did you know my size?' she asked curiously, through the closed door, shivering despite the warmth of the atmosphere, as Mel's voice fell on her ears like the touch of a velvet glove.

'Oh, that wasn't a problem,' came his airy disclaimer. 'What I've chosen for you would fit anyone.'

'I'm not ready to come out just yet,' she called back hastily. 'Can you just hand it in to me?' She sheltered behind the half-opened door, extending her hand in the direction of his voice, wondering what on earth he had chosen.

'Why not?' A large bag emblazoned with the blue Ulysses butterfly logo was deposited in her hand. 'I got it from the resort boutique.'

Carefully Kerry opened the bag and drew forth a fine cotton fabric patterned with scarlet and salmon pink hibiscus blooms interleaved on a pale turquoise background.

'Oh, it's a sarong! How fabulous!' she exclaimed, shaking out the rectangular length of cotton, impressed with the colour and vibrancy of the print and the quality of the fabric. 'Why don't you go up to the Beachcomber Bar and wait for me? I'll try a few experiments, and when I think I've found the style which suits me best I'll come along and ask for your opinion.'

She held her breath, fearing he would invade her privacy, knowing that if he did she would repulse him then and there, and the evening would be over before it had begun. Surely she was entitled to a few more hours of the subtle magic which had coloured the day? She had promised him nothing.

'OK, if that's the way you feel, sweetheart.' To her relief, he accepted her decision without demur. 'I booked a table for eight. That should leave you plenty of time.'

She heard the doors open and close, counting to five before she emerged into the main room. Thick curtains gave her all the privacy she needed, while the ceiling fans moved silently but efficiently, cooling the air as she folded and tied the soft material in different ways.

It took her an hour before she'd settled on a style which really suited her slender but curvaceous figure. The one problem was that, because it left one shoulder bare, she wouldn't be able to wear a bra beneath it. So what? It was a warm night and the fabric was substantial enough to save her from blatant immodesty.

With careful fingers she retied the relevant knots, swathing the cotton tightly round her hips, emphasising their youthful slimness and elegant shape. The lower edge of the garment touched her legs at mid-calf, balancing the bare-shoulder look, and highlighting the gracefulness of her body. Luckily she had just the right sandals to wear with it. Gold strap, with tiny heels, so insubstantial that she had been able to pack them easily.

She made up her face with competent fingers, conscious that she couldn't allow the vibrancy of the dress to overshadow her. Boldly she increased the allure of her eyes, delighted when she could find a lipstick which toned perfectly with the pink hibiscus blossom. How about her hair? She thrust her fingers through it, lifting it upwards and holding it in a bundle on her crown.

It wasn't a style she normally favoured because of the tendency for wisps to escape and look untidy, but tonight was different. Tonight she needed something special. She took her time and, using clips, she formed her tresses into a coronet of red-gold. Staring at her reflection, she felt a wave of surprise wash over her. How different she looked, and it wasn't just the make-up or the new hairstyle. Wonderingly she touched her parted lips, feeling their warmth. Was this what being in love did for a woman? If it was, then her sophisticated dinner companion would read just how badly she was suffering from the malady!

Her pupils darkened. For him to see her naked soul would be as humiliating as if she were to display her naked body to him when she knew his interest in her was only physical. Tonight she would have to walk a tightrope. She would take what was her right—the right to enjoy the facilities of a resort where she had booked and paid for her own holiday—but avoid displaying the cheaper tricks of a courtesan out of a sense of self-esteem, although it was in that role that Mel McKinley had cast her! At least, she consoled herself, she wouldn't be the first woman to suffer from unrequited love. As Mel himself had said, time would cure her.

Outside the cabana it was dark, the scent of jasmine in the air, the soft sound of the sea a murmur in the distance. Here and there trees were spotlighted, massive shapes stirring in the evening breeze like ancient gods surveying their kingdom. Dear heaven! The whole place was enchanted, and she was caught in its spell for better or worse. Her mind shied from the evocative words. There would be no promises at the end of this night.

Shortening her stride to match the inhibitions of the binding sarong, Kerry began to walk along the main pathway which led from her cabana towards the Beachcomber Bar. She was so intent on keeping her eyes on the dimly lit path that when a tall figure loomed out in front of her she gave a gasp of shock and surprise.

'Kerry—it's me!' Mel took her by the arm, staring

down into her face. 'I got to thinking I should have waited on the veranda and escorted you, rather than letting you find your own way.'

'I took longer than I anticipated.' She licked lips which were parched, tasting the subtle perfume of her own skin. 'What do you think of the dress?'

'I have no words to describe you. . .' His head moved in silent negation. 'What is it about you, Kerry, that makes the adrenalin rush to my veins?'

'Irritation? Contempt?' she suggested, her smile hiding the hurt that still lingered because he might desire her but he still didn't trust her integrity.

'Don't spoil it,' he warned softly. 'Whatever's happened in the past, whatever will happen in the future, this night is meant for us. Every hour, every moment. . .and we're going to wring every last drop out of them, so that when we're old and grey we'll look back on this day. . .and smile into our bedtime cocoa.'

The breath caught in her throat as his intensity reached across the small space between them, and she felt an answering echo begin to build deep inside her. This way lay peril!

'I don't. . .' she began, determined to keep the conversation light.

'Drink cocoa,' he finished for her, an odd note in his voice. 'But there's one thing at least that you do very well, my beautiful little liar!'

Before she could protest he had drawn her into his arms, sliding his hands down her back, pressing her form against his own so that she had to raise her hands to his shoulders to save herself from stumbling backwards.

'Don't make me take your lips, sweetheart, give them to me,' he murmured thickly. 'I've been on my best behaviour ever since we left that wretched golf course, and the strain is beginning to tell.' His mouth found her cheek, drifted to the corner of her mouth as she struggled in his hold.

'Mel. . .don't! Please don't!' It was her own reaction she was rejecting as well as his obstinacy in seeing her as a sparing user of the truth, but the distinction was lost on him.

'Relax, Kerry. I'm not going to whip you back to the cabana and make you miss dinner, partly because when I make schedules I don't rearrange them unless there's an emergency, and partly because once I have you to myself I don't mean to hurry events.'

He was so close to her, she was devouring the essence of him—the scent, the feel, the taste of him—and it was driving her crazy. As if under a powerful hypnotism, she obeyed him, seeking his mouth with her own, sighing as he possessed it with strength and gentleness, enfolding her to his body as his hands stroked her back through the brightly glazed cotton of her sarong.

She felt her body go limp as he slowly brought the powerful kiss to a conclusion, as a final touch, brushing her lips with the tip of his tongue.

Now was the time to tell him that she had no intention of consoling him for his loss of Belinda. Now! Before he read her silence as complicity. But the words of rejection wouldn't form. How could they, when every fibre of her body was on fire for him?

'Time to leave, sweetheart,' he told her softly, his voice husky and coloured by a hint of self-mockery, as his lips drifted from her skin. 'Before this situation turns into an emergency and one perfectly good dinner reservation bites the dust.'

CHAPTER TEN

THE food at Banfield's was just as excellent as Kerry had expected—the atmosphere quietly intimate, encouraging the exchange of confidences, as Mel played the perfect, considerate host. Yet despite his projection of coolly civilised man, she found it impossible to ignore the undercurrent of tense emotion which charged the atmosphere around them, or to forget the sensations his last passionate embrace had engendered within her.

Would he resent her questioning him further about his early life? she wondered, disturbed by the shimmering air of expectant silence that hovered over them, and as anxious to break the build-up of tension and the way her errant thoughts kept straying to his earlier promises as to learn more about him.

'Are you still in touch with your mother?' she asked tentatively, as she finished the deliciously thick barramundi steak she had chosen as her main course.

'We keep up the formalities,' he replied easily. 'Both my sisters are married now, and I went over to New Zealand for their weddings, but the atmosphere was rather strained. I'm still regarded as something of a black sheep, I'm afraid.'

'After everything you've achieved?' Kerry was astonished.

Mel shrugged. 'I'm tarred with the same brush as my father was—chasing financial success at the expense of family life—a maverick, unsettled existence.' His strong, beautifully formed mouth turned into a reluctant smile. 'At least they can't accuse me of having abandoned my responsibilities as my father was supposed to have done.'

'People's values are different.' Kerry searched his face,

reading the allegiance to his father's actions despite their results. 'Some women would be prepared to put up with their husbands' preoccupation with business, particularly if he was building up a future for his family.'

'Would *you*, Kerry?' He raised his wine glass to his mouth, watching her over the rim.

'I think so, yes,' she said honestly after a few moments deliberation. 'It might not be easy, but if I loved someone, then I hope I would understand that he had other needs beside mine.'

'As you understood your mother's needs?' he asked softly, leaning forward across the table, his expression enigmatic.

'I suppose so.' She stared at him, unseeing, his face a blur against the dim lights. She'd never consciously considered her mother's needs, responding automatically to the older woman's vulnerability, being strong where Louise had been weak, assuming authority where her mother had faltered.

'And Murray's too?' he enquired softly.

Kerry shook her head. 'How could I? No, my decision to come to Australia was purely selfish. I suppose you could equate it to the need of an adopted child to find its parents. I needed to find out as much as I could about Warren, my father.' Her voice changed, became husky with uncertainty. 'To be honest I was scared witless when I arrived on Murray's doorstep. My mother had always told me how uncaring he had been towards us. I was quite prepared to be rejected out of hand.'

'Instead?' Mel queried softly.

Kerry's lovely mouth parted in a smile of utter happiness. 'Instead he was so close to tears it was almost embarrassing!' she confessed. 'Not for me, but for him. It wasn't that he hadn't cared for us, but he hadn't been able to come to terms with the tragedy of Warren's dying so young. By the time he did, Mum had returned to England, having taken me with her, convinced that

Murray hated her.' She shook her head wonderingly. 'He was too proud to try and resume contact with us, and he'd become resigned to never seeing me again.'

'Yeah—he was quite ecstatic about your return to the great Australian Davies clan.' Across the table Mel's eyes lingered disturbingly on her mouth. 'I remember hoping at the time that he wasn't expecting too much.'

'And was he?' she challenged, her mouth going suddenly dry as she sensed with dismay the disapproval echoing in his lazy drawl.

'That remains to be seen,' he mused indolently, his eyes mercilessly intent on her expectant face. 'He would certainly be shaken if he suspected your generous nature extended to consoling married men whose wives happened to be unavailable because of their advanced pregnancy.'

Shock mingled with indignant anger as Kerry stared at his grim face. Her first impulse was to rise from the table with elegant dignity and sweep out of the restaurant leaving him to pick up the bill, but her limbs seemed curiously heavy, unwilling to obey the urgent summons of her mind. With that cruel, unjustified gibe he had destroyed the whole ambience of the evening. Beneath his intent regard she could feel her heart pounding as an angry tautness held her immobile.

'Yes, I'm sure he would,' she concurred tightly when she had rediscovered her voice, deliberately keeping it toneless. 'Neither would he approve of one of his drivers forcing himself on one of his hostesses, would he?'

'Albioni forced you?' His elegant eyebrows lifted.

'Not Nick! You!' Power had returned to her limbs, and Kerry rose, pushing her chair back, wanting only to escape. 'You've forced your unwelcome company on me from the moment we left Cairns!'

'Unwelcome?' His voice was low and intense, throbbing with a barely controlled anger. 'You have a funny way of demonstrating your displeasure at times!'

'What do you want me to do? Hit you on the head with my plate?' she bit out, feeling the adrenalin flow through her veins and shaking with the effort of controlling her voice, incensed even more because she recognised the justification of his retort.

'And become the centre of a public disturbance?' He was angry too, but it was the alert anger of a big cat biding its time to strike. 'Try it if you like.'

'Your head's not worth the destruction of the china.' She looked down her pretty nose at him, half of her regretting the bitter end to which the evening was drawing, the other half glad of the escape it offered her. 'And now, if you don't mind, I'm feeling a little tired, so I won't wait for dessert.' Holding her head high, she rose to her feet.

'Kerry!' Mel thrust his napkin down on the table, and was at her side before she could blink. 'This is absurd! You asked me a question and I gave you an honest answer. If I'd known you were merely seeking compliments. . .'

'I wasn't.' Clear and cool, her voice was deliberately devoid of emotion. 'I wanted the truth as you saw it. Where I went wrong was hoping that you'd realised by now just how myopic your judgement was. You've never been interested enough in my opinion to ask me what I think about you, but I'm going to tell you anyhow.'

She drew in a deep breath to stop her voice from shaking as his brow furrowed darkly. 'You're a man whose life is ruled by expediency—who takes what he wants where he wants when he sees it, who lives for the day and damn tomorrow! A predator who kills for pleasure, a hunter who stalks the weak. Well, there's one thing you ought to know! One day tomorrow will come and you'll regret all the todays when you were too hubristic to exercise a little understanding. . .a little charity. . . Perhaps in view of the recent upheaval in your personal life you already do——'

Her voice broke as she attempted to evade him and make for the door. 'Unless you want to end your life a lonely old man, I suggest you stop taking stock of the McKinley company, and start taking stock of Mel McKinley himself!'

She had half expected him to prevent her leaving the restaurant, but he stood aside as she brushed past him, and she only had time to register the hard set of his jaw coloured by the deep flush of anger and the hard brightness of his icy eyes before she felt the welcoming cool breeze of the tropical night on her own heated skin.

'Wait!'

She had hesitated only a few seconds to get her bearings, but he was at her side, grasping her shoulder with harsh fingers.

'Let me go!' Too near to tears, she wouldn't apologise for a word. She had struck back to wound his pride as he had wounded hers. If he smarted, she was glad! But the dreadful irony was that, because she loved him, she was forced to share the pain she had inflicted.

'Kerry, listen! We have to talk. . .'

Did she detect a note of pleading in his rough retort?

'Hi, Mel—they said I'd probably find you here!'

'Susie?' Mel muttered something unintelligible under his breath as one of the resort hostesses strode briskly out from the shadows.

Pretty and blonde, her curvaceous body attractively displayed in the resort uniform, she gave them both a broad smile. 'No probs, honey. Just a phone call from Cairns for you. Lady said it was urgent.'

'Damn! OK, Susie. Hold her on, will you? I'll be there in a moment.' He waited until the girl had moved away on her errand before taking Kerry's other shoulder with his free hand. 'It's probably the receptionist at the hotel. One of our brood must have left something behind. . .'

'Then you'd better go and sort it out. Do something

you're really good at.' With a sudden spurt of energy
Kerry wrenched herself away from his predatory hands.
'And when you've sorted it all out find somewhere else
to spend the night, because I intend to lock my door!'

Her eyes, now accustomed to the gloom, had discerned
the path she needed, and she made her escape from him,
running as fast as her slender heels and confining sarong
would allow her. She half expected to hear the thunder
of his heels behind her, but there was nothing. Back at
the cabana her hand shook as she opened the door.
Inside she carried out her threat, locking it firmly and
drawing the curtains across.

She ached all over, and her body, primed for pleasure,
wept its disillusionment. Stumbling to her bed, she lay
down on it, drawing up her knees and hugging them.
She had undoubtedly lost her job, but that was the least
of her worries. She doubted if Mel would ever forgive
her. Certainly he would never understand that her attack
had sprung from the deep fount of love for him she had
discovered within herself, because she would never be
able to embarrass both of them by declaring it.

Some time during the night the weather changed.
Kerry, whose emotional exhaustion had carried her to
sleep faster than her troubled mind could have hoped
for, was awakened by a crash so loud that she sat upright
in bed, clutching the light cover to her chest, her heart
pounding with fear.

It took a few moments to realise that the steady drum
of sound which had replaced the soft silence of the tropic
night was torrential rain bouncing off the corrugated
roof of the cabana. As for the crescendo of noise which
had brought her to sudden wakefulness, well, it must
have been a coconut torn from the branches of a nearby
palm.

Shivering from the shock of her rude awakening allied
to the sudden drop in temperature, she glanced at the
adjacent bed. Now that her eyes had grown accustomed

to the gloom she could see it was empty. Where on earth would Mel be? she wondered guiltily. The luminous hands of her small travelling-clock showed her it was four in the morning. Had he returned to the cabana? She thought not. If he had come back determined to claim his bed, she was sure he would have found the means of awakening her. Alternatively he would have asked at the reception desk for another key. No, it seemed he had obeyed her instruction and found some other place to spend the night. But where?

It took an hour before she drifted back into sleep, and by then the force of the rain had lessened. At half-past seven when she awakened again the sun was shining from a clear sky, and the only evidence of the night's storm was the lingering scent of the tropical vegetation.

Well, since she had finally got what she wanted, she would have to make the best of it! Forcing Mel's image from her mind, telling herself that, whatever fate had overtaken him last night, it was none of her concern, Kerry dressed herself in jeans and a T-shirt, and clipped her hair at the back of her neck with a large clasp. She then made her way to the restaurant.

'Hey, Kerry! Come and join us! Charlie's in the queue for toast!'

It was Kylie, already devouring cereal and milk with bacon and eggs standing by, who hailed her.

Glad of the company, Kerry helped herself to some rolls and marmalade before filling her cup with delicious aromatic coffee from a nearby jug and pulling out an empty chair. Some time she would have to come face to face with Mel, she knew. The more she could delay that encounter the happier she would be!

'You missed a great evening,' the older woman told her cheerfully. 'There was a talent competition in the lounge after dinner, and afterwards a group of us went back to one of the other cabanas and had a game of cards. Shame about your migraine—it can be a real curse, can't it?' She tut-tutted sympathetically. 'Glad to see you're looking great this morning.'

'Yes, the attacks don't last long.' She returned Kylie's smile. So that was how Mel had explained her absence! Whose face was he trying to save? she wondered.

'Has Mel told you about the arrangements for today, love?' Kylie cleared a space on the table as her husband joined them.

'Arrangements? No—I——'

'Haven't got round to it yet.' The deep voice at her shoulder made her start so that coffee spilled from her cup into the saucer.

He looked handsome and composed, and wherever he had spent the night it hadn't been out in the open, as she had half feared. He was groomed to perfection, his chin smooth, his jeans and navy T-shirt spotless. He would have had time to slip into the cabana to change after she had left, but not to shower and shave. Clearly he had found facilities elsewhere to perform those functions! Her relief was mixed with irritation that on the evidence his night had probably been less disturbed than hers!

'I've already made my own plans for today,' she lied quickly.

'Postpone them, then.' Across the table Mel's grey eyes held her attention as he gave the laconic instruction. 'You won't want to miss this.'

'Mel's got a mate in Mission Beach with this great racing yacht,' Kylie interjected eagerly, 'and he's bringing it across so's we can go out to the fringe reef and snorkel!'

'Oh!' Pride fought with longing as Kerry's pulse quickened. She'd been aching to snorkel again after her baptism at Cairns, and as for a sailing yacht. . . The prospect was decidedly tempting, if only she hadn't resolved to keep Mel McKinley at a distance.

'But the weather. . .the storm last night. . .' she prevaricated, unwilling to give a definite answer beneath Mel's mocking gaze.

He raised lazy shoulders. 'Wind's veered and fresh-
ened a little, but there won't be any difficulty in finding
a sheltered beach on one of the islands. 'Believe me,
Kerry, it's something you shouldn't miss.'

'Not afraid of the sea, are you?' It was Charlie,
speaking for the first time, his brow wrinkled with
concern.

'No—no, it's not that. . .' She bit her lip. Impossible
to explain why she was so reticent about sharing yet
another day in Mel's company. On the other hand, she
wouldn't be alone with him. Kylie and Charlie would
make excellent chaperons, and then there was Mel's
friend, too. What really surprised her was that Mel
should still want her with him after the things she had
said to him the previous evening.

She cast a doubtful look at his face, but his expression
was bland. 'That's settled, then,' he said cheerfully.
'Now eat up. We have to be down by the jetty at nine.'

From the moment Kerry saw the fifty-two-foot *Seahorse*
any reservations she harboured about her change of heart
vanished.

The magic of the reef, the sense of freedom that
exploring the coral gave her, the delicious, tropical
smorgasbord that the taciturn but friendly Reg prepared
for them on board while they explored the small island
of Coombe, the leisurely conversation—everything was
faultless, and if her heart ached every time she dared to
fill her eyes with the sight of Mel McKinley's beautiful
hide, and her pulse raced each time his grey eyes
acknowledged her presence there, then it was a small
price to pay for the ephemeral enchantment.

As the afternoon drew to a close, she left Kylie and
Charlie sunbathing on the beach and Mel in conversation
with Reg, and made her way to the isolated tip of the
island. Here, with the waves crashing and sucking at the

rocky shoreline and the huge outcrops of sun-and-sea-polished granite towering above her, the sense of isolation was complete.

'Beautiful, hmm?'

She hadn't heard Mel's approach and, for an instant, as she turned sharply she felt resentment that her seclusion had been interrupted. Her foot slipping on the smooth rocks, she would have fallen if he hadn't moved swiftly in his rope-soled trainers to steady her.

His strong arms enfolded her while she regained her balance, and every trace of pique vanished as she became aware of the heat of his sun-soaked body, the salty tang of his bare skin and the quickened beat of his heart. Apart from the trainers the only item of clothing he wore were brief bathing-shorts, and she was unbearably conscious of the attraction of his lean body, the deep-tanned flesh, the developed muscles of his chest, as he pulled her hard against himself, seeking and finding her mouth with his own, possessing it with a swift urgency that was irresistible.

The heat of his thighs burned into her own bare flesh, her breasts, cramped against the hard wall of his naked chest, stung with tumid protest as a deep internal warmth which had no claim against the tropic sky surged downward through the sensitive tissues of her woman's body, as his tongue invaded the sweet cavern of her ceding mouth. She had spent nearly a full day in his company, but this was the first time they'd been alone. He'd taken her by surprise, and her traitorous body had succumbed to him of its own volition.

'Does this mean I'm forgiven?' he murmured shakily, his hand caressing the silky skin of her back where her low-dipping one-piece exposed it.

'I—I. . .' It was difficult to speak because although he had finally released her mouth his lips were moving in a gentle path across her cheek, paying tribute to its warm softness.

'I didn't hear you apologise,' she said at last, desperately aware that it would be madness to deny her absolution when her body, shivering and pulsing beneath his caresses, told its own story.

'The words don't come so easily,' he murmured against her skin. 'That's why I brought you here. I only invited Kylie and Charlie because I thought you wouldn't come if it was just the two of us. It was the only way I could think of persuading you to share some more time with me, to give me a chance of putting the record straight.'

His mirthless laugh echoed in the stillness surrounding them. 'I spent last night worrying in case you did something rash like taking the water-taxi to Mission Beach first thing this morning and phoning Murray, demanding he sent out a rescue squad to collect you.'

That's what she should have done, of course. Now it was too late. With her body so close to Mel's that her heartbeat seemed to be echoing his own, and her thighs tingling deliciously as the soft fuzz of his upper legs rubbed against them, she knew she would never find the resolve to leave him.

'Where *did* you spend last night?' she asked curiously.

'Ah. . .' His mouth found the hollow of her shoulder and impressed its softness there.

His reluctance to supply an instant answer roused her suspicions. A vivid picture of Susie, her familiar greeting announcing a long-standing friendship at the least, flashed across her mind.

'Susie,' she said flatly. 'You spent the night with Susie.'

'Yeah.' He stood back, moving his hands to hold her wrists. There was no trace either of shame or apology on his unsmiling face as his clear grey eyes met hers with only a hint of challenge. 'She overheard our parting words, and since we knew each other from way back she

offered me shelter in her cabana on the staff estate until
you cooled down.'

His expression or Susie's? Well, what had she
expected? Mel had been frustrated, and one bed must
have seemed like any other when it was occupied with a
willing female form.

'I see,' she said stonily, trying not to show how his
admission had swept the sunlight from the sky for her.

'Do you?' His mouth tightened as he stared down at
her clear eyes. 'What do you see, Kerry? An orgy of
lovemaking while the palms shuddered and the sea
boiled? Because if you do, you're doing both of us, Susie
and me, a grave injustice. Susie offered me the hand of
friendship because she knew there was no question of
my abusing it. Her job would have been on the line if
anyone had found out and reported the instance, because
the staff quarters are away from the main resort and the
guests aren't welcome there.'

Confused by the turmoil of her reaction, Kerry tried
to regain her lost ground. 'I didn't mean to imply. . .'
she began.

'Oh, yes you did, sweetheart!' The gleam in his eyes
impaled her. 'And I'm very glad you did, because now
you should be able to understand why I was so unreason-
able about you and Albioni!'

'You mean—at last you believe what I told you?' Was
this what he'd meant about putting the record straight?
The shock and relief were so great she could do nothing
but stare back at him, praying she had read his meaning
correctly.

He nodded. 'The truth is my judgement of you was
warped from the very first moment I learned of your
existence, because Murray came on so hard about you at
a time when my feelings towards all women were somewhat jaded. I couldn't believe such a paragon of beauty,
intelligence and charm really existed, and to be honest I

resented his obvious intentions of bringing the two of us together.

'Then, when Albioni told me the two of you were lovers, I thought my worst suspicions had been confirmed, and I saw red. Not only because it broke the company rules, or because I knew Murray would be disappointed in his new-found idol's association with a married man, but because if there weren't the single people around to encourage the married ones to forsake their families, more children might grow up knowing both their parents!'

'Oh, Mel. . .' She couldn't be angry with him. On the strong male face with the hard bones of an adult man she could see a trace of the boy who had lost contact with his father because a rich single man had offered his mother another haven.

'Logic told me it was in your interest to plead ignorance for the sake of keeping your job and staying in Murray's favour,' he was continuing in a low voice. 'But as the days went by instinct suggested you were telling the truth, and suddenly I found myself wanting to believe Albioni had tricked you into becoming his lover, and that now you knew the facts you'd be able to throw him out of your heart as I hoped you'd throw him out of your bed!'

His mouth moved ruefully in a grimace of despair. 'Then last night I blew the whole thing because I was devoured by jealousy, still haunted by the fact that you were only here with me because I'd spoiled your original plans.' His bitterness lay like a barrier between them, as Kerry struggled for words to express her understanding. 'I never intended to ruin your holiday, Kerry.' There was no mistaking the thread of sadness that subdued his soft drawl. 'I can only hope today has made some amends for what I've put you through.' He paused as his eyes dwelt lingeringly on her. 'On a personal basis I never had the right to judge you or subject you to physical harassment——'

'Mel, please. . .' She started to speak, shocked by the sudden emptiness of his expression.

'No, Kerry,' he interposed gently. 'Let me finish. There's something else. While one part of me wanted you to have been an unwilling victim of Albioni's lies, there was another part which wanted you to be the amoral flirt he suggested.'

Silently Kerry shook her head as a cold wave of nausea brought a shudder to her warm skin. 'I don't understand,' she whispered, appalled.

'Sweetheart. . .' It was the first time he had given any meaning to the word which had tripped so easily from his smooth tongue. 'I'm no saint, but even I couldn't live with myself if I seduced Murray's ewe lamb. So from now on the cabana's yours and yours alone. When Reg sails back to Mission Beach I'll be on the *Seahorse* with him.'

'No!' Overcome by horror, there was no way Kerry could control her startled outcry, as all her accumulated feelings came to a head. 'I don't want you to go, Mel!'

Jealous, he had said. A primitive masculine emotion, but surely one that showed he cared a little for her?

'I was angry yesterday. . . The things I said. . .' She winced as she recalled her furious words. 'I was just striking out, trying to hurt you as much as you'd hurt me!'

She watched him swallow. Saw the fitful movement of the larynx in his strong throat.

'Forget it, Kerry! There was a lot of truth in what you said. Apart from that, I've no right to be sharing your cabana, but I can't impinge on Susie's generosity for another night.'

'You don't have to. Not while there are two beds in my cabana,' she offered breathlessly, all her desire for him shining in her hazel eyes, darkening them to moss velvet. 'Couldn't we make a fresh start?'

Slowly Mel shook his head. 'It wouldn't work,' he said softly, his voice deep and husky. 'Because I can't give you my promise that I wouldn't try to seduce you.'

The emotive words hung between them. He didn't love her, but surely she had enough love for both of them? Oh, how she ached to hold him in her arms, restore his faith in women, comfort and console him for all the other unfaithful women in his life. Give him her body as a symbolic token of her love, asking nothing in return, so that when the time came for him to return to the mainland some of his bitterness would be healed. She could never hope to compensate for the loneliness of his childhood, or replace the love he'd lost when his father died or Belinda left him, but she could repair some of the damage, couldn't she? Every fibre of her body assured her that she could, every pulsating nerve and throbbing blood vessel urged her to try.

'Kerry?' He'd been watching the fleeting shadows cross her expressive face, the shining honesty reflecting in her eyes, the tremulous movement of her soft mouth still damp from his kisses. Her name, spoken in such a low tone that it was barely audible, contained both question and plea.

She drew in a deep breath, knowing that what she was about to say would have an effect on the rest of her life.

'It would work, if you want it to, because I wouldn't ask any promises from you.'

For the briefest instant their gazes clashed, then she was clasped hard against his chest. She laid her head on his shoulder, unable to refrain from tasting the salty dampness of his skin with the tip of her tongue, her heart filled with joy, her mind empty of regrets. She had fought against this decision for so long, yet it had been inevitable, and somewhere deep inside her subconscious she had known it, if not from the first sight of him, then from the first touch of his mouth on her own.

'We have to go.' It was several minutes later when he reluctantly released her, his expression wry. 'Reg wants to start back for Dunk soon.' He sighed against her hair. 'If you only knew how much I'm regretting that we're not the only two people here.'

'I can guess.' His body had shared its secrets with her, and he could hardly be unaware of her own state of physical arousal. Lifting one hand, she traced his profile with a loving finger. 'But we soon will be alone together, won't we?'

CHAPTER ELEVEN

'OH, KERRY, my love. . .'

As soon as they entered the cabana and she slid the door shut behind them, she was in Mel's arms, achingly aware of his need for her, her inexperience no bar to her natural response.

'My love', he had called her. From Mel it was just a term in his vocabulary of seduction, and she had to bite her tongue to stop herself from pouring out her own feelings, betraying her ingenuousness.

He was muttering endearments, his words fragmented as he interspersed them with tender kisses. She could feel the warmth of his body communicating itself to her, lulling her fears, arousing an answering fever as she strained against him, seeking the hard outline of his desire, accommodating it in the cradle of her own trembling body.

His mouth caressing her face, his hands began to explore her, following her curves with hands which moulded and excited her, sliding inside the loose T-shirt with which she'd covered her swimsuit, to stroke her naked flesh with a reverent hand which left a trail of heat in its wake.

There was a kind of awe on his serious face, and he swallowed deeply, his pupils darkly dilated in the dim light, as his hands divested her of the unwelcome clothing, moving to the soft swell of her breasts in their thin nylon covering, cupping them in his palms as his thumbs trailed delicately across her soft nipples. Fierce trails of sensation sped through her nervous system, causing her to gasp as her body reacted to his touch.

Instinctively, blindly she reached for him, sliding her

hands beneath his protective shirt as he had done with
her, breathing her pleasure in soft sighs as she felt the
hot silk of his skin quiescent beneath her fingertips,
suddenly conscious of the demands of her own body—
the rising surge of heat, the aching yearning that drove
her to seek comfort against his hard arousal.

His groan of delight thrilled through her, lending her
courage to become more bold. With bated breath she
reached for the waistband of his shorts, feeling and
exulting in the shudder which racked his expectant form.
He moved away from her for just as long as it took to
dispose of his clothing, then he was peeling away the
pretty swimsuit from her own eager body.

'Kerry, sweetheart,' he murmured, 'this day has been
the longest in my entire life.'

'Mine, too,' she said breathlessly, consumed by an
internal fire as his hands travelled avidly over her bare
skin, exulting in her new-found power as his potent body
hunted against hers with a new and primitive urgency.

With a groan of impatience he lifted her off her feet,
laying her gently on one of the beds, following her down,
leaning across her, his face darkly intent.

Touching the heated dampness of his chest, fingers
sensitive to the soft hair that grew there, Kerry became
more audacious, running her seeking hands down his
body, enjoying the spasmodic movement of his muscles
beneath her caress, encouraged in her exploration by the
unrestrained pleasure of his reactions. The golden fuzz
on his thighs was not harsh at all, but springy and soft.
She sighed in satisfaction at the knowledge as it tickled
her tender palms, holding back her impulse to bury her
face in its softness.

It was only when his predatory hands slid further
down her body that she felt a tremor of alarm. This was,
after all, the time she was about to yield her virginity. It
should be a simple and painless process. She was young
and athletic, wasn't she? But Mel knew nothing of that.

He might have absolved her of condoning adultery, but he hadn't actually said he accepted her denial of being Nick's lover, had he? Frantically she cast her mind back to what he had said on Coombe. It was possible, probable even, that he thought her sufficiently experienced to know what she was doing, despite the fact that he had exonerated her from being a party to Nick's deception. A small spark of fear ignited in her mind. In comparison with her female form Mel was brutally powerful, superior in height and weight and muscle.

'Kerry, what is it?' She heard the uncertainty in his voice, and knew he must have sensed her sudden mental withdrawal.

'Nothing really.' She was finding it difficult to find the words she needed to explain the chaotic emotions which were tormenting her. 'I haven't. . . I don't. . .' Miserably she fell silent.

Then she heard his soft laugh. 'Oh, sweetheart—I thought you'd changed your mind. There's no need for you to worry about anything. I'll take full responsibility for protecting you.'

'Oh!' Her hands risen to hold his shoulders tightened in shock. Fool that she was, she hadn't given a thought to such things! A cold sweat broke out on her face. Never in her life had she acted with such total irresponsibility. Suppose she had become pregnant? At least she wasn't so stupid as to think it couldn't happen the first time. Too many girls had consoled themselves with that specious thought and lived to regret it. Her only excuse was that she had acted on the spur of the moment. Love had befuddled her, obliterating reason, leaving only emotion and sensation. . .

'Give me a few seconds. . .' He moved away from her, and she knew that, if she had any second thoughts, now was the time to voice them. He wouldn't like it, but he would accept her decision. If she could doubt that, she wouldn't be loving him as much as she did.

She stayed silent, accepting him as he returned to her arms with a small sigh of pleasure. Whether it was his consideration for both their well-beings—especially hers—or the sheer physical rapture of reuniting her flesh to his she didn't know, but in that moment of synthesis all her reservations disintegrated. In a movement as old as time itself she invited him to find his pleasure and his solace in her hot velvet fastness.

'Hold me, Kerry, help me,' he whispered, strangely humble. 'Show me how much you want me.'

With a sense of exultation she obeyed him, caressing him until she sensed the moment was right for both of them before guiding him towards fulfilment. With a cry of triumph he took her, easily, without trauma, thrusting into her warmth, his strong male body homing in triumphant pleasure.

At first she made no movement, content to feel his possession, joyously aware of the pleasure she was giving him, deeply psychologically fulfilled by the knowledge that she was taking his strength and beauty within herself, and that for the rest of her life nothing would obliterate the memory of her first lover.

Traumatised by the tempestuousness of the act of love, it was several moments before she was able to relax mentally enough to give as well as take. Then, almost without being aware of it, her hips began to move, finding a rhythm to oppose Mel's so that each powerful thrust he made was intensified.

At what point she finally lost control of the situation she never knew. The moment when her mind blacked out and her senses held sway would always remain a mystery to her. She just knew that when Mel had said she would fly before the holiday was out, he hadn't just been referring to parascending. Then, just when she thought she could stand the mounting pressures of her own body no longer and began to cry out unintelligible pleas for help, her world exploded into a haze of the most exquisite pleasure.

It took a little while for it to come back to its axis, and when it did she was aware that Mel was still hard and wanting, kissing and murmuring unintelligible words into her ears, that somehow he had controlled his responses to her internal rhythm, and now it was her turn to give him the sweet release which had been his gift to her.

She took her time, her sole aim to please him, her heart bursting with love, so attuned to his responses that when she felt him plunge into a suddering explosion of ecstasy she began to weep, her hands stroking his shoulders while she murmured comforting words as she would have done to a baby.

For a few moments he collapsed in total weakness against her, his breath sawing, his chest rising and falling so violently that she feared for his life.

'Mel. . .darling?' She placed her hand on his heart, alarmed by the power of its beat. 'Are you all right?'

He moved slightly, bearing his own weight, but leaving his limbs entwined with hers. 'More than all right,' he assured her, cupping one of her breasts with a hand, but refraining from caressing it, as if he knew instinctively that every part of her anatomy was so sensitised that even the light sheet was an impossible burden on it. 'And how about you, Kerry?'

He was regaining control of himself, and now she could hear a hard edge of anger in the question he posed.

'I'm fine,' she whispered. 'Why wouldn't I be?'

There was a short silence, then he said simply, 'Because this was a new experience for you.'

'Does it matter?' She sensed his concern and was frightened by it. They should be spending the rest of the night in each other's arms, not holding a post-mortem on her experience. . .or lack of it! 'Someone has to be the first.'

'But not that swine Albioni!'

She wouldn't have been human if she hadn't experienced a glow of pleasure that she had been so completely vindicated.

'I'm surprised you realised.' Her voice trembled. 'I didn't think I was that. . .green.'

'Oh, Kerry, sweetheart,' he sighed. 'You supplied a mixture of clues from the first day I met you, only I was too pig-headed to acknowledge them. Of course,' he said after a long pause, 'Albioni gets his cards the moment I get back to Sydney.'

'Oh, no! You can't do that!' Shocked, Kerry raised her head to stare down at his unrelenting face. 'Think of his wife and children—the new baby. . .'

'Why?' he demanded icily. 'He didn't. What would have happened if I hadn't slapped a suspension on him for speeding? Would he be the man in bed with you now?'

'Of course not! How can you suggest such a thing?' She was horror-stricken that he could even contemplate such an event after what had just happened between them. 'Perhaps he misread the signals I was giving out— mistook friendship for something more. But once I'd put him straight he wouldn't have forced me. I've worked with him quite a long time; I know!'

'Do you?' His face was hard to read in the darkness, but his voice left her in no doubt as to his feelings. 'I doubt that very much. The guy didn't even have the guts to tell me you knew nothing about the arrangements he had made on your behalf.'

'He would have been afraid of losing his job,' she interjected hurriedly. 'I don't suppose for a moment he guessed you'd go through with the idea of taking over his accommodation when he told you he was my lover.'

'That's no excuse for maligning you.' His gaze sharpened. 'Don't tell me you still feel something for him after all the trouble he's caused?'

'Of course I don't!' she protested crossly. 'And I resent your implying that he could ever have replaced you! Look, Mel. . .' Her tone softened. 'I'm here with you, because I. . .' Abruptly she paused. She'd been going to say 'because I love you'—but that could spoil everything. Love had never been mentioned between them. Smoothly she found an alternative ending. 'Because I want to be. If you'd been Nick Albioni, you'd be spending the night on the veranda—or, if not, *I* would be!'

She sighed as he remained silent. 'Nick's an opportunist, but he's not evil. He wouldn't have hurt me, and if it hadn't been for him we wouldn't be here now together, would we? You can't punish him for that.'

'Wrong, sweetheart! I can damn well do what I like,' Mel said curtly. 'So let's call the argument closed, shall we?'

On the point of remonstrating, Kerry kept silent, counting to ten instead. She'd made her opinion known, there was no point in locking horns with Mel McKinley—she'd never won any battle between them yet, and she had plenty of time left to persuade him to change his mind. And if she failed, then she would have to concede victory to him, and hope that Nick's expertise would soon get him another job, and that his wife would never learn of the reason behind his dismissal. The decision was Mel's by right, she conceded, and there was a poignant sweetness in the knowledge that he was prepared to shoulder major responsibilities without being swayed by outside influences, even if in this instance she wished he would show a little mercy.

'If that's what you want,' she said sweetly, smiling in the growing dusk, and receiving the consolation of a deep, tender kiss for her surrender, as her unforbearing lover turned and took her in his arms.

* * *

It was half-past nine before they had breakfast the following morning—just managing to get into the restaurant before it closed. Afterwards they sat by the three-tiered cascade pool, enjoying the brilliant sunshine, cooling off periodically by plunging into the cool, refreshing water.

Her hazel eyes protected by sunglasses, Kerry lazed back on her sun-lounger, filled with a happiness made more intense because of its impermanence. Who would ever have thought that she would fall in love with Mel McKinley? Yet, from the start, there had been that spark between them, arcing with the force of a short-circuit. She'd thought it had been dislike. Now she knew she had been wrong. On her part, at least. She turned her head slightly so that she could observe his profile. Like herself, he was wearing sunglasses, so it was impossible to know if he was awake or asleep. He really was a beautiful man. His body firm and virile, his muscles smooth and well developed—the result of hard work and natural exercise, she thought, rather than applied training, but that alone didn't account for her loving him.

As for his feelings about her—just how deep did they really go? He found her attractive enough to take her to his bed, but he'd never said he loved her—but then neither had she declared her feelings for him in those terms. She knew so little about him really—just that potted history of his early days and what Murray had told her about him. That plus the fact that he was a tender and considerate lover. . .and that Belinda Fraser must have been mad to have abandoned him.

'Go on—ask me, then.' He turned his head lazily in her direction, and she realised that he'd been conscious of her appraisal all the time.

Ask him if he loved her? Never!

'I was wondering what plans you had for this afternoon,' she prevaricated.

'That depends if you'd prefer to spend it indoors or

outdoors,' he said softly, placing a lazy hand on her thigh.

'Outdoors, I think,' she said after due deliberation, well aware of what he was asking her. There was something about pacing oneself, exercising self-control that made the eventual culmination that more rewarding. Mel had taught her that by turning the previous day into one long experience of mental foreplay.

He nodded, at ease with her decision. 'How about a leisurely walk through the rainforest to Coconut Beach? We can take a picnic with us instead of having lunch here, and eat it beneath the shade of the calophyllum trees when we arrive. It's about an hour's walk and well worth the effort.'

'It sounds lovely,' Kerry agreed enthusiastically, not at all sure what a calophyllum tree looked like, but satisfied with the information that it provided shelter from the tropical sun.

'Right! I'll try and organise some food and drink for us.' He rose to his feet, six feet plus of superb male, totally unselfconscious of the honed perfection of his body covered only by brief bathing-trunks.

'Shall I come with you?' She began to rise, but he pushed her back gently.

'No. Reserve your strength, sweetheart. I don't want you so exhausted at the end of the day that you fall asleep on me.'

'Suppose you fall asleep on me?' she asked, allowing herself to be resettled on the sun-lounger with no protest. Truth to tell she was quite happy to stay where she was, hugging her secret to herself. The secret that her body still retained the impression of Mel's possession, the imprint of his body within her own. Close her eyes and concentrate, and her tissues told her that they remembered his hardness and his domination.

Mel removed his sunglasses, regarding her with sparkling grey eyes. 'That's about as unlikely as the Coral Sea

freezing over in midsummer,' he boasted. 'Don't expect
me back too soon. While I'm up I'll go over to the sports
complex and book us for horse riding tomorrow
afternoon.'

'If you insist.' Kerry leaned back on her lounger,
turning her face towards the sun. She'd never been on
the back of a horse before, but if Mel recommended it,
then she was sure she could cope. With a sigh of utter
contentment, she relaxed, closing her eyes, allowing her
other senses to satiate themselves with the sound of the
sea-birds, the soft cooling breath of the breeze and the
scent of tropical flowers.

'Excuse me, I'm looking for Mel McKinley. I understand he was here a while ago.'

At the sound of a female voice in close proximity to
her, Kerry sat bolt upright, her eyes focusing on the slim
figure of a woman probably a few years older than
herself, wearing a simply styled but obviously expensive
fuchsia-pink silk dress. Another of Mel's friends from
time past?

'Yes. He's just gone off to make some arrangements
for the rest of the day,' she offered with a smile. 'He's
probably somewhere between the restaurant and the
sports complex at the moment, but he should be back
here soon.'

'I'll wait here for him, then, if that's all right?' The
newcomer sank down on the sun-lounger recently
vacated by Mel. 'I asked at the pool bar, and they said
you'd probably know where he was.' She smiled, a
lovely-looking woman with smooth blonde hair caught
back in a bandeau and falling to her shoulders. 'My
name's Belinda Fraser. . .' She paused, then stretched
out her left hand on the third finger of which a scintillat-
ing diamond sparkled with almost vulgar vigour. 'I'm
his fiancée. He may have mentioned me.'

'Yes, yes he did.' Innate politeness forced Kerry's
answer even while her world crumbled around her.

Belinda here? And claiming to be engaged to be married! 'But I thought, that is. . .' She faltered, hearing again Mel's voice, terse and harsh, assuring her that what had once flared between himself and this beautiful socialite had been reduced to ashes.

Belinda uttered a soft laugh, stretching her arms above her head and easing her muscles like a Siamese cat. 'You heard about me and Mel splitting up?'

Still reeling from the shock of her shattered dreams, Kerry could only nod her bright head.

'A storm in a teacup.' The blonde shrugged shapely shoulders. 'Pre-wedding nerves start early when you come from a family like mine. Honestly, I think it would be simpler to organise a coronation!'

She drifted ice-blue eyes over Kerry's rigidly held body. 'They told me at Reception Mel had been sitting here and *you* might know where he was.' Her voice indicated only polite interest.

'I——No, that is. . .' Kerry's world was falling apart, but that was no reason why she should disillusion her companion. The poor girl didn't deserve to know that her errant fiancé had been finding his own amusement in her absence. She swallowed, retaining her self-control with a mighty effort. 'I work for Metline,' she explained steadily. 'I was Mel's hostess on the tour he brought up to Queensland, and we had some spare time before the return journey——'

'Yes, he told me when I phoned him from Cairns the evening before last.' She smiled the smile of a beautiful woman who was very sure of herself and her hold over the man she wanted. The smile of a woman who would never see a humble, plain little tour hostess as a rival, fortunately for Mel's peace of mind; and she would be quite right.

'You mean he's expecting you?' The words burned in her throat as Kerry recalled all too clearly Susie's summons to the telephone.

'Actually, after I'd put him out of his misery we arranged to meet at the Mission Beach resort at the beginning of next week, because I had to make a duty call on my grandmother first. But frankly, it was so deadly boring I decided to cut it short and surprise Mel, so I hired a plane, and *voilà*! Here I am!'

She looked around her with interest. 'It really is quite pleasant here, isn't it? You can't believe how frustrated I was when I arrived in Sydney to tell Mel that he was forgiven, only to learn that he'd suspended one of his drivers for some traffic misdemeanour and had decided to take the tour to Cairns himself!'

'It must have been quite a shock.' Her mouth dry as beached coral, somehow Kerry managed to make a polite response. Oh, Mel, how could you? Inwardly she wept. How could you make love to me when your Belinda had come back to you? How could you do that to either of us?

'Oh, I'm used to his unpredictability! And, of course, he was in a pretty bad state at the time.' Belinda seemed totally unware of Kerry's frozen expression. 'He took our row pretty badly, and I guess he had to work it out of his system somehow. Anyway, it worked out quite well really, because I decided to visit my grandmother and put Mel out of his misery at the same time.'

She settled more comfortably on the sun-lounger, undisturbed by Kerry's silence. 'So when I phoned the hotel in Cairns where the tour generally stays, and they told me he'd come over here for a few days' holiday, I gave him the glad news. As a matter of fact——' she leaned forward confidentially '—I think I know why he came here rather than staying on the mainland.'

'Do you?' How easy it would be to shatter her companion's complacency. How easy—and how impossible!

The other girl nodded. 'Mel came here with his father some years ago, and he told me he thought that Dunk would be the ideal place for a honeymoon. I guess he was just wallowing in his misery—dreaming of what might have been. Only now, of course, it can be.'

Kerry nodded. If only Belinda knew to what extremes Mel had gone to exorcise her memory, she would probably throw his ring back in his face!

Between herself and Mel McKinley there had been no promises, no undertaking. He had lusted after her, and she had given in to that lust without conditions, because she loved him. No, it was worse than that! She had begged him to stay with her when he had already told her he was going back to Mission Beach with Reg!

Oh, dear God, she had thrown herself at him, and he had accepted her offer with all the casual desire of a virile adult man!

'We usually go to Hayman Island in the winter, but I think Mel's probably right. This has something different to offer.' Belinda cast another charming smile in Kerry's direction, seemingly oblivious of the distress her revelation had caused the other girl. Stretching out her slim, tanned legs in front of her, she continued smoothly, 'I hope he's not going to be too long. I've got to be back in Cairns by late afternoon. Some ex-college friends of mine are giving a party for me, and I'm hoping to take Mel back with me. We can drive down to Mission Beach later, to celebrate our reunion. After all, there's no point in his staying here now all by himself, is there?'

'Of course not,' Kerry agreed, wondering if she would ever find the strength to stagger to her feet and flee from this nightmare.

'He should be back any time now,' she forecast, her eyes turning with a hunted desperation in the direction of the sports complex, praying for a quick end to her ordeal and being instantly rewarded. 'Ah. Here he is now!'

It was the stimulus she needed to get her on her feet, gathering her towel and high-factor sun-cream with agitated fingers, her anxiety to escape this torture now a driving need.

'Oh, please don't go on my account!' Belinda's innocently lovely face beseeched her.

'I must. There are things I have to do.' It was an effort to speak, but Kerry was proud of the act she was putting on when she was falling apart inside. 'Besides, Mel won't want me here when he sees you!' She left at top speed, the other girl's protestations still echoing in her ears.

CHAPTER TWELVE

DAMN him! Damn Mel McKinley for being two-faced. How could he condemn Nick when he was just as ready to default on a vow?

Kerry hadn't expected much from him. Only that he'd finished with one affair before starting another. More fool she. If she'd known he was contemplating marriage again she would never, never have had anything to do with him! Never have cheapened herself or allowed him to cheapen his mended relationship with Belinda. . .

Instinctively she made for the cabana, sliding the door open, regaining its coolness and throwing herself face down on the bed. Too shocked to cry, she lay there silently, flinching only when she heard the mournful, unfinished cry of the lonely kookaburra who, with the irony of fate, appeared to have found a perch on the papaya tree outside.

Mocked by a bird, she thought listlessly. That was what her soaring dream had descended to. There must be something intrinsically wrong with her, or did other women find themselves inevitably attracted to rotters? She only knew she had to escape while Mel was still enjoying his reunion with Belinda—go somewhere where there was no chance they would see each other again before he left the island with Belinda.

Of course, she would have to resign from Metline; her position would be untenable there in the circumstances. Little wonder Mel had reacted so angrily against Nick when he'd discovered that she was a virgin! Seducing Murray's granddaughter when he supposed she was experienced was one thing—becoming her first lover was something else!

167

Not that she had any intention of discussing the matter with her grandfather! She was, after all, a consenting adult, and had to take her share of the blame for what had happened. In view of the castles the older man had been building in the air, Mel would be likely to find himself on the end of a stock-whip—for the second time in his life!

She managed to smile at the picture that thought created as her fighting spirit reasserted itself. She was wounded, but she'd live to fight another day, wouldn't she? Her mind made up, she changed her swimsuit for shorts and a T-shirt and marched out of the cabana, her head held high.

By accident rather than design she found herself passing the deserted clearance in the garden where guests were invited to dehusk any coconuts they found lying around.

On impulse she seized one and, using the technique Mel had explained to her the previous day, brought its lighter end down on the raw metal spike provided for the purpose. Nothing happened, but she wasn't going to give in so easily. All her disappointment, all her anger at the abrupt dissolution of her dreams, gathered in a hard knot of aggression. Time and time again she lifted the coconut above her head, smashing it down on the spike. Feet splayed, arms rigid, she used every atom of her strength, and was soon rewarded by a tearing noise as the first shards of the outer case splintered.

Teeth gritted, feeling the cool perspiration running down between her breasts, she vented her feelings in a show of controlled aggression, breathing harshly, every nerve and sinew concentrated in achieving her end, ripping the loosened husk away from the inner nut until triumphantly she held it in her hand.

'Right,' she said softly between her teeth, holding the dehusked nut on high. 'This is Mel McKinley's head, and this is what I'd like to do with it!'

With hard, efficient swings she brought the widest part of the circumference of the nut into contact with the edge of the brick, turning and smashing, turning and smashing until, with a satisfying crack, the nut broke into two perfect halves, revealing its milk-white heart.

'There!' She surveyed the result with some pride, aware that the muscles of her upper body were protesting at the violence of action she had forced upon them.

'Congratulations!' The voice was unmistakable as the figure of the man she loved moved from the thick, concealing bushes of the surrounding rainforest. Apparently completely immune to her cry of shock and her horror at seeing him, he moved smoothly across, taking her right arm in a firm grasp to lift it high above her head. 'I give you Kerry Davies—a new British and all comers' record in coconut dehusking!'

'Take your hands off me!' Furiously, she wrenched her arm out of his grasp, taking several steps away. She'd thought most of her pent-up anger had been dissipated, but she had been wrong.

'Hey—sweetheart. . .' Mel held up both hands, palms towards her. 'It's me—the guy you're sharing your holiday with. . .remember?'

'Yes, I remember!' Her tone was clipped, her voice betraying an icy dislike. 'And don't you dare "sweetheart" me! Didn't Belinda tell you she and I have been exchanging confidences?'

She watched his jaw harden, the smile leave his eyes. 'Yeah—she mentioned it. What exactly did she tell you?'

'You mean you don't know?' Her eyebrows lifted contemptuously. 'Well, your fiancée was very eager to tell me how she had decided to forgive you and wear your ring again. She also told me that she'd phoned you and broken the good news to you two days ago!'

'Now listen to me, Kerry,' Mel's mouth was a steel trap, his eyes arctic-cold.

'No!' she interrupted fiercely. '*You* listen to *me*! I

spent last night with you because I wanted to, but only because I thought you were free to indulge your—your. . .'

'Carnal appetite?' he suggested softly, his eyes narrowed now, surveying her with a deadly purpose. 'Do go on.'

Her head lifted proudly. 'Carnal appetite, then.' She accepted his phrase and his invitation to continue. 'But you weren't! Belinda trusted you.' She hefted in her breath, allowing the coconut halves to fall to her feet as her fingers balled into closed fists in anguish. 'How do you think she would have reacted if I'd told her you and I were lovers? That you'd never volunteered any information about your reunion—that you'd let me believe that she was no longer any part of your life?'

'Why didn't you?' He was regarding her as if she were something unpleasant that had crawled out of the undergrowth, and she could hardly credit his question.

'Certainly not for your sake,' she returned tartly. 'Obviously your opinion of women is pretty grim. I would never deliberately hurt another woman just for the sake of it. Perhaps someone should warn her about your irresponsible behaviour, but it wasn't going to be me! You may have treated me with contempt, using me as a convenient instrument for your—your. . .'

'Lust?' He was too calm, totally without shame, but Kerry was too enraged to marvel at his reaction.

She inclined her head in a sharp nod, accepting his own terminology. 'You treated me in a most humiliating way, as a one-night stand. I didn't expect love, I'm not that gullible, but I was stupid enough to believe, to hope, that you cared something for me personally, that at least I had won your respect. . .'

She had already said too much, betrayed her susceptibility. Clamping her lower lip between her teeth, she tried to regain her composure.

'You're quite wrong, you know, sweetheart,' he

drawled, his face still that mask of indifference. 'It wasn't a one-night stand I had in mind—more like a fourteen-night one, only you passed out on the first occasion before I could have my wicked way with you.'

'It's not a laughing matter! You've behaved abominably!' God knew what she'd expected from him, certainly not humility, and he was confirming her expectations in that respect.

'Who's laughing?' He took two steps towards her, and she backed further away, finding her passage blocked by the trunk of a large tree.

Clasping her hands behind her back, she rested against it, glad of the support as her legs threatened to collapse beneath her.

'I see I've got to explain the facts of life to you, sweetheart,' Mel was continuing grimly, for the first time allowing the mask to slip, to reveal his growing temper. 'And since I anticipate that's going to take some time, I suggest we go back to the cabana. I'm not used to brawling in public.'

'Like hell, we will!' Kerry refused to be cowed by the undercurrent of violence she could now detect in his bearing, the taut body, the slight flush on his taut cheekbones. She doubted it anybody had taken Mel McKinley to task for many years, and he clearly didn't appreciate the experience. 'There's nothing you could tell me that I want to hear!' she retorted vigorously.

'Don't be too sure of that,' he smiled knowingly, his eyes still sharp points of aggression. 'For example, if I were you I'd take my hands away from that tree pretty damn quick.'

'Why?' Her natural caution made her obey him. Bringing her hands forward, she found they were acting as hosts to quite a few green ants. 'Oh, I'm not afraid of ants,' she dismissed the intruders airily. 'They're not doing any damage.'

'That's because they're not angry,' Mel said briskly.

'Anger can turn the most docile creature into a raging predator—as I have reason to know.'

Before she could prevent it, he had taken both her hands, brushing off the invaders with swift, effective movements.

She didn't believe a word of it. It was just another pretext to gain superiority over her, and it wasn't going to work, and as for that dig about angry predators—if it had been aimed at her she had every right to be angry! On Belinda's behalf even more than her own. He should be thanking his lucky stars that his fiancée hadn't discovered his infidelity.

'There's nothing I want to discuss with you at all,' she said briskly. 'The sooner you get on that plane with Belinda the happier I shall be! At last I'll be able to enjoy this holiday instead of being perpetually harrassed!'

'Stop being a little fool, Kerry.' His hands descended on her shoulders, his fingers predatory as they tightened to shake her with controlled violence. 'I've had just about enough of this nonsense! It's time. . . Yow!' He broke off, uttering a yelp of anguish.

Wide-eyed and not a little concerned, she stared at him as he released her shoulders to examine one of his wrists. 'Little bludger bit me!'

Wonderingly she gazed at the soft skin of his inner wrist where a tiny green body could be seen firmly fixed in a vertical position, its pincers deeply locked into the flesh as its body rocked backwards and forwards with vicious enthusiasm.

Fate had a strange way of repaying debts, she thought, refusing to feel sorry. It wouldn't be a lethal wound, and if it hurt only half as much as her broken heart did, then he'd escaped lightly! More to the point she'd been offered an opportunity to escape from his haranguing as he concentrated on removing his solitary attacker, his brow frowning in concentration.

'Pity it wasn't a python!' she said scathingly, and took to her heels.

He didn't follow, and after a while she slowed down, finding herself on one of the many winding paths of the resort garden. What should she do now? Looking towards the coast at the fast ebbing tide, she suddenly knew the answer—Mung-um-gnackum!

Cautiously she made her way back through the resort towards the air-strip, following the runway until she was able to climb down to Pallon Beach.

The reef was already well exposed as she began trudging across the water-logged ground in the direction of the small island. At first the going was easy, although it was far from the smooth sandy surface she had expected. Instead she found herself walking on chunky rock formations not unlike what she supposed the surface of the moon to be.

Only as she grew nearer to her destination did she experience a few qualms, as the reef became so covered with large black sluglike creatures about twelve to fifteen centimetres in length and thick as two plump pork sausages, with skins like polished, embossed leather. Her progress became very slow as she had to put each foot down with great care and plan a pathway some time in advance to stop treading on them.

It was with a feeling of relief that she eventually saw the reef give way to fine sand and she was able to reach her destination without further problems.

As Kerry explored the island she wondered idly how many people ever troubled to visit it, with its twisted mangrove trees, and stretches of pure white powdered sand. Flinging her arms wide, she allowed the light breeze to caress her, lifting her hair, teasing her skin—the moment some compensation for the pain in her heart.

Later, sitting down on the beach, she rested her hands on her knees, gazed out at the coast of Dunk, and allowed the silence of her surroundings to embalm the misery of her spirit. She would survive. If Dunk could flourish again after devastation by cyclone, then the heart of Kerry Davies would heal in time, she told herself firmly, and wished fervently that she could believe in her own optimism.

Not having a watch with her, she was uncertain as to how long she sat giving herself up to the healing powers of nature, but she hadn't opted out of society sufficiently not to keep an eye on the tide, and there was still no sign of its return when she decided she'd communed with nature long enough to allow for Mel and Belinda's departure and the time had come to return to civilisation.

From the other side of Mung-um-gnackum she had seen the golden causeway of sand she had hoped for stretching towards Pallon a hundred metres or so further up the coast. The return journey should be a lot faster, she opined hopefully, and not nearly as traumatic as having to avoid the enormous sea-slugs which had plagued her outward trek.

So it proved. On a few occasions she was passed at great speed by something which appeared to rise out of the sand and flash past her at thigh-height. Puzzled, she was left with the impression of a fish of some kind, diamond-shaped, rather like a skate with a long tail. But surely skates were deep-water fish? She shrugged the matter aside, her mind too full of unhappiness to dwell on the problem.

Walking slowly along Pallon beach to where the path from the airport strip descended to the sand, she heaved a sigh. What would Mel be doing now, she wondered bitterly? Drinking champagne in Cairns?

'You crazy little fool!'

For a moment she thought she was hallucinating, as a figure came leaping down the sand dunes backing on to the airstrip to take her forcefully by the shoulders.

She'd never seen Mel McKinley in such a temper. Not

even when she'd confronted him with his treachery at the dehusking centre.

'Haven't you learned anything about this country yet?' he demanded forcefully. 'Don't you know you never go anywhere on a place like this without telling someone where you're heading, in case of trouble? Look at you!' His gaze seared her with furious intensity. 'No water with you, no sun-barrier cream, no watch!'

'I didn't take a map either,' she volunteered drily. 'I thought as I could always see Dunk from offshore, I could get back to it without a compass.'

'Very amusing!' His tone told her he found it anything but. 'Lady, I've got news for you. You're not in a leafy England lane now. These are the tropics and they have to be treated with respect.' He glared at her tightly mutinous expression. 'Even in these idyllic waters, there may still be a few nasties lying in wait for unsuspecting tourists who don't know how to protect themselves.' His eyes flicked to her feet. 'At least you wore thick soles. They'd probably protect you if you stood on a stone fish, and there's no danger from marine stingers at this time of the year, but what if you'd disturbed a basking sea-snake, or been lashed by a sting-ray?'

'A sting-ray?' she faltered, a horrible thought occuring to her.

'This place is famous for them.' He regarded her thoughtfully, reading her dismay. 'In fact, the reef round here is known as "sting-ray reef". They bury themselves in the sand at low tide, with just their eyes protruding, and woe betide anyone who disturbs them.'

'They're poisonous, then, are they?' she asked in a small voice, shuddering as she recalled those flying bodies with their whiplike tails.

'Deadly if you're a small sea animal,' he told her with some pleasure. 'Fortunately they don't hunt us. They're more anxious to get out of the way of marauding feet, but if one of those barbed tails struck you by mistake

you'd know it. The sting's painful enough, and can cause
palpitations and a feeling of nausea. On someone more
than normally susceptible, the effect could be very
serious indeed—particularly if they found themselves
paralysed with the tide coming in!'

'You're trying to frighten me!' White-faced, Kerry
challenged him.

'Better frightened than drowned!' There was no
remorse in Mel's tone, and Kerry looked away rather
than meet the icy censure of his cold stare. 'If you
wanted to scare the living daylights out of me, sweetheart, then you've succeeded, but you might have spared
a thought for Murray. Losing his son was bad enough
without depriving him of a granddaughter because you're
too dumb to see the truth when it's staring you in the
face!'

What truth? From the expression on his face Mel was
in no mood to provide an answer.

'How did you know where I was?' she asked instead.
'And why are you here, anyway? Shouldn't you be on
the mainland by now?'

'An ancient instinct handed down by my aborigine
forebears,' he mocked her. 'As a matter of fact, I asked
around at the resort when I could find no trace of you
anywhere. I'd hoped you'd had the common sense to tell
someone where you were headed, but no. In the end it
was the pilot of a helicopter doing pleasure-trips round
the islands who provided the clue. He'd seen a lone
walker making for Mung-um-gnackum.'

He regarded her with little pleasure. 'My search was
over and, as for the other answers you wanted, I'm here
because your safety was my first concern, and because I
never had any intention of going to Cairns with Belinda.'

'I didn't mean to worry anyone,' she told him thinly,
holding on to her pride with an effort. Suddenly she felt
very tired.

'We'll sort that one out at the inquest.' Grey eyes

surveyed her from head to toe. 'At the moment you're suffering from a surfeit of sun and dehydration. The sooner I get you back to the resort the better!'

To her astonishment, he picked her up in his arms and turned towards the air-strip.

'You can't carry me all the way!' she cried, feeling the powerful beat of his heart against her cheek, and fighting the urge to cry.

'I shan't need to.' He breasted the rise, and she could see one of the resort jeeps parked on the road which ran alongside the runway. 'I borrowed transport from one of the gardeners.' He cast her a look of glowering grimness. 'I had no idea of the state you'd be in.'

'I'm fine!' she protested as she found herself thrust down unceremoniously on one of the hard seats.

'Enjoy the feeling,' Mel told her tersely. 'It may not last long. Here, take a drink of water!' He handed her a cooler-wrapped bottle, and she drank gratefully.

Mel drove with angry speed, which, since they were the only traffic on the road, was excusable. By the time he'd parked the jeep on the nearest road to the cabana, and pulled her unresisting form into its fan-cooled atmosphere, her previous light-headedness had disappeared.

'Right, sweetheart.' He turned a face like thunder in her direction. 'Sit down and listen to me!'

'There's nothing to discuss. . .' she began contentiously, determined not to let him get under her guard. He looked big and strong and lovable, and she was so near to breaking-point. It would be so easy to fling herself in his arms and apologise for all the trouble her little excursion had caused, but the retention of whatever scraps of pride she had left was paramount.

'Kerry,' he said slowly, 'in normal circumstances I'm not a violent man. But you have the ability to set my adrenalin racing, and I'm just about at the end of my tether. So I'm advising you—sit down while you can still do so comfortably.'

Her mouth opened and shut in amazement. He was actually threatening to beat her! And by the look on his face it was no idle threat. Normally she would have protested with some acidity, but in this case she sensed that discretion was the better part of valour. She sat down.

'OK,' he nodded approvingly, coming to stand in front of her, glowering down at her upraised face. 'Let's not beat about the bush. I am not, and have never been, engaged to marry Belinda Fraser.'

CHAPTER THIRTEEN

'OH!' IT was all Kerry could say, apart from calling him a liar, and that seemed definitely inadvisable under the circumstances. Both his blood and his temper semed to be running high, which was not surprising if he had spent several hours in the heat of the afternoon scouring the resort for her.

'Belinda told me. . .' she ventured carefully, when it seemed something was expected of her.

'A whole packet of lies, apparently.' Mel thrust his hands deep into the pockets of his shorts. 'Sure, I knew her socially. She moved in the same circles as my father in Perth, but we never had much to do with each other until my father died. He left a large gap in my life. . .' He looked at Kerry, his eyes sharp with aggression, as if he expected her to mock his vulnerability.

'I can imagine,' she said softly, and saw him relax.

'Yeah—well. I got to thinking about settling down, raising my own dynasty. I was the last McKinley, and someone had to carry on the coaching tradition. Belinda was the obvious choice, the *only* choice at that time, because I'd spent so much time working I'd left myself very little time for leisure.'

He started to prowl around the room, while Kerry remained silent, a tiny bud of hope stirring into life deep within her.

'She seemed—fond—of me,' he said at last. 'Because her social routine was as hectic as my round of work, we'd never spent much time alone together, so I decided to take time off, relax, get to know her better. That was when our names began to be linked together by the media.'

179

Again he paused, staring out at the fading light.

'Gradually I came to realise that the image she presented to the world was all a sham,' he said at last. 'Beneath that civilised exterior she had no idea of what loving was all about. Used to having her own way, she was merciless with anyone who opposed her. The more time I spent with her the more aware I became of her shallowness, the importance she gave to inessentials, her pretentiousness with people she liked to term her friends. I realised then that, far from growing to care for her, I didn't even particularly like her. Believe me, it was a disappointment as well as a shock when the scales finally fell from my eyes.'

'I'm sorry.' It was barely more than a whisper, as Kerry saw the reason for his bitterness through new eyes.

He gave her a brief smile. 'It's not easy for a man of my age to admit he's been a fool, and I decided to steer clear of women rather than make the same mistake again. That's when I decided to go to Sydney and sort out our Metline connection. Believe me, the last thing I wanted was to have another candidate for marriage thrust at me! Especially by a man whom I held in great respect, and whose feelings I didn't want to hurt!'

Kerry shook her head sadly, unable to prevent the warm colour that rushed to her cheeks. 'In all honesty, Murray's matchmaking was none of my doing! I'd no idea what he was up to at the time. Even when he suggested I work for Metline when I said I wanted a job, I thought it was because of my previous experience in the hotel trade. If I'd known what was in his mind I would have thought twice about stampeding your office. I must have been the last person you wanted to see!'

'You were.' Mel smiled with real humour gleaming in his eyes as he sank down on the other bed, facing her. 'But you were the first person to rouse me out of the torpor of self-pity I'd sunk into. A little busybody of an

English madam, full of her own importance and her relationship to my fellow director, trying to put the world to rights.'

'Is that really the impression I gave?' Kerry asked, chagrined. 'At the time I thought I was fighting for a just cause.'

'Just or not, I decided you needed a lesson, and I was just the man to be your instructor. As far as I was concerned, you'd arrived out of the blue, taking poor Murray by storm, and using your influence with him to get a job for which you weren't qualified!'

'But I went to the training school!' she protested quickly.

'Unfortunately Murray had neglected to mention that fact, and I'm afraid I just jumped to conclusions because I was pretty disillusioned with the female sex as a whole at that time. Anyway, that's when I got the idea of taking the coach up to Cairns myself. There's nothing like a change of job to revitalise a man, and the physical and mental effort of driving a coach all that way, and the responsibility it entails, would be just the challenge I needed, and at the same time I could put you through your paces.'

'I was pretty horrified when I found out,' Kerry admitted. 'I thought you were going to make my life impossible.'

'Did I?' He leaned forward, transfixing her with his grey-eyed stare. 'It was never my intention to victimise you.'

'No.' She had to be honest with him. She owed him that, particularly after what he had told her about Belinda, although there was still plenty she didn't really understand in that situation. 'You were very fair—except when you accused me of making eyes at Colin.'

'Jealousy,' he told her succinctly. 'The old green-eyed monster, my love; because you see, Kerry, I'd discovered the woman who possessed the fire and the spirit I'd been hungering for all my life, but the damnable thing was she was deeply embroiled with another man—or so I thought. A man who already had two children and whose wife was expecting a third!'

His eyes slid over her face, the irises smoky with a deep-felt emotion. 'I'd tried to fit Belinda into the pattern of the woman I thought I wanted as a wife, and she'd failed miserably, and now here *you* were! Totally unsuitable for my pre-arranged plan, and I was aching to possess you with every fibre of my mind and body!'

'Oh, Mel. . .' Kerry said in despair. 'I can see how bad it looked to you, and what you must have thought, when I made no objection to your taking Nick's place!'

'A mixture of elation and disgust,' he admitted ruefully. 'Although if I hadn't been so full of myself and my own needs, I wouldn't have been so dumb as to doubt you. I've never met a girl with more honesty shining out of her eyes.'

'Really?' she asked in a small, choking voice. 'I must be a very bad judge of character myself, because I believed every word Belinda said this morning.'

'She's a practised liar,' Mel said sadly. 'At first I used to think it was just white lies that came so easily to her lips, but as I grew to know her better I realised she manipulated people just for pleasure. Despite her veneer of charm and beauty she's motivated only by wealth and maintaining her position within the social circle she graces.'

'And you were never engaged to her?' Kerry had to ask him, although he had already denied it.

'Never,' he said emphatically. 'I was never in love with her, I never asked her to marry me, and I never bought her a ring. As I said, as soon as I realised there could never be a future for us, I told her I intended to spend some time on the eastern seaboard, and that it would be for the best if we didn't resume going out socially on my return. I told her my business commitments made too much a demand on me to continue being a satisfactory escort.' He gave a deep sigh. 'Perhaps I should have been more brutal with her, but at the time it seemed the right way to do it. A way to save her pride, particularly as the media seemed bent on seeing us as a twosome. Let her friends think that in my absence she had deserted me rather than the other way round. . .'

'She had this beautiful ring. . .'

'Look at me, sweetheart.' Mel took her face gently between his two hands. 'I don't blame you for doubting me—God knows, I doubted you enough and without such good reason—but I swear to you that I've told you nothing but the truth. Belinda's father made a million in the timber industry—she has a jewel-box full of ostentatious rings. Not one of which came from me.'

'She must have loved you very much to follow you here.' Kerry looked down at her hands, sympathy washing over her for the other girl, who had everything but the love of the man she wanted.

'Save your pity, sweetheart. Belinda doesn't know the meaning of the word "love",' Mel retorted drily. 'Pique, yes. She's used to calling the shots, and she didn't take too kindly to being shunted to one side. It seems I fitted the prototype of the man she envisaged as a husband, and she was confident enough to imagine she could persuade me to resume our association. In her world there are very few things that money allied to beauty can't buy.'

'So when she phoned you. . .?'

Mel shrugged broad shoulders. 'She just went on as if nothing had happened. Whether she thought she was irresistible, or whether she wanted me back so that she could break with me at her own place and in her own time—to refute the gossips who were whispering that I had been the one to walk out—I don't know.

'Hell, Kerry!' he muttered, thrusting one hand into

his hair in a sharp gesture of irritation. 'I was in a furious temper, anyway. I'd just managed to ruin our evening because I hadn't been able to control the niggling jealousy which was etching away inside me, and I'd no idea how I was going to make amends for my stupidity. I wasn't in any mood to play games with Belinda! I told her the truth: that I had met someone else and that we were staying here together.'

'So you didn't have any intention of meeting her in Mission Beach?' she asked unevenly, the tender plant of hope beginning to grow and unfurl its tender shoots.

'Of course not.' He denied it flatly, his mouth clamping shut with the strength of the denial. 'She did suggest it, but I told her once more that I had no plans to see her again, and put the phone down.'

'But she still came here?' Kerry raised puzzled eyes to Mel's stern face.

He exhaled heavily. 'As I said, all her life she's been used to calling the shots in her relationships. I don't think she ever envisaged a situation where she couldn't use either her looks or her father's money to get what she wanted. When she realised that I couldn't be manipulated she wanted the last word. No matter how much it cost her financially, she wanted to cause me trouble in revenge for the humiliation she considered she'd suffered at my hands. At least, that was the impression she gave me during a short but vitriolic exchange of views!'

'She must have thought a tour hostess easy grist for her mill,' Kerry acknowledged with a wry smile. 'She certainly sent me running!'

'Not as far and as fast as I dispatched her!' Mel's voice hardened. 'And this time with no possible misunderstanding about my opinion of her and the wiles she employed.' He sighed. 'The only thing in her favour was that she probably thought you were some kind of transient affair.'

'Aren't I?' Kerry's voice trembled so much that the words were barely distinguishable.

'Don't you know yet?' Mel swung his strong body off the bed, and knelt at her feet. 'You're my first and only love, Kerry. My flame and my desire. My present and my future. If I have to spend the rest of my life driving around Australia with you as my hostess until I can persuade you to make Murray's dreams come true, then that's what I'll do.'

She only had to look at his face to know he was speaking the truth.

'Murray's dreams?' A wave of emotion so pure, so exciting, so utterly incomprehensible swept over Kerry, so that she felt more drunk that she had the evening of the Dunk Island milkshakes. 'What about yours?'

'Have you *still* not realised that over the past weeks they've become identical?'

'Oh, my love, my dearest love. . .' She ran her fingers through Mel's thick hair, lifting his face so that she could pin butterfly-kisses on his mouth, his cheeks, his nose, hardly able to credit what she was hearing.

'So will you make us both happy men?' He was surprisingly humble, apprehension clouding the faultless grey of his eyes. 'I want to spend the rest of my life with you, Kerry. I knew it as a certainty that night in Cairns when you soaked yourself and the whole hotel bedroom, but like a fool I refused to admit it to myself.'

'But you still believed then that Nick and I were having an affair. . .'

He nodded. 'I hated the thought of it, but I still loved you. God knows, I'm no saint. I had no right to judge you.' He slanted her a wry smile. 'And knowing that made me angrier still, because suddenly I couldn't control my own emotions. So will you be my wife?'

'It's not necessary. . . I mean. . .' She saw his brows draw together, and stumbled on unevenly. 'I mean, not just because of last night. . .'

'Not because of last night,' he agreed huskily. 'But because of all the days and nights to come when I want you beside me sharing my life.'

He paused, sombre eyes dwelling on her face. 'Give me the chance to make amends for the tough time I've been giving you, show me your compassion, and love me a little, Kerry, and I'll do my best to make that little grow. . .'

She shook her head, her heart flaming with the joy of his declaration, saw his mouth tighten in pain, and rushed into words to alleviate it.

'I couldn't love you more than I do already, Mel!' The relief of saying the words was enormous. 'Even when I was furious with you I still loved you, although it took a little time before I realised what was happening to me!'

'Ah. . .' With a harsh murmur he drew her to him, his eager hands lucid messengers of the desire which transformed him from supplicant to predator. 'It's a lot more than I deserve, but I'm not going to question my good fortune. . .'

As he sought her parted lips with his mouth, Kerry gave herself up willingly to his demanding fervour, drawing his hard man's body into the soft comfort of her own complementary curves, exulting in the evidence of his need as his breath quickened and his heart thundered against her own, knowing she had truly come home.

It was more than an hour later when, naked and relaxed, she rolled out of Mel's encompassing arms and asked hopefully, 'Are we going to eat tonight?'

'The food of love isn't enough for you, sweetheart?' He raised a lazy eyebrow.

'I missed lunch,' she said apologetically. 'Besides, I really should phone Murray. He'll be wondering how I'm enjoying myself. I said I'd keep in touch.'

'Good, then you can tell him our news.' His eyes gleamed with amusement. 'His approval is a foregone conclusion—with the prospect of his great grandson or granddaughter having a directorship of Metline in the future.'

'You don't intend to change the name to McKinleys eventually?' she asked in surprise.

'Why should I?' He seemed genuinely surprised. 'It's a fine name with a fine tradition behind it. And tomorrow I'll phone the operations manager in Sydney, and have him fly another hostess up for the return tour from Cairns, because I don't intend to let you out of my sight until you wear my wedding-ring. Then, for the remaining days, you and I will have a trial honeymoon—and, if we find it satisfactory, we'll come back here and repeat the experience after we're man and wife. Any objections?'

'No.' Kerry gave him her most limpid smile, all her hopes and expectations locked into that one word. 'None at all.'

Outside on the papaya tree, the kookaburra's bright eye caught the unusual sight of a dipping blue wing in the fast-approaching dusk and, recognising a potential mate after months of deprivation, threw back his head and laughed—the full, descending, joyous chuckle of his species.

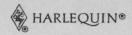

The most romantic day of the year is here! Escape into the exquisite world of love with MY VALENTINE 1993. What better way to celebrate Valentine's Day than with this very romantic, sensuous collection of four original short stories, written by some of Harlequin's most popular authors.

**ANNE STUART
JUDITH ARNOLD
ANNE McALLISTER
LINDA RANDALL WISDOM**

**THIS VALENTINE'S DAY, DISCOVER ROMANCE
WITH MY VALENTINE 1993**

Available in February wherever Harlequin Books are sold. VAL93

COME FOR A VISIT—TEXAS-STYLE!

Where do you find hot Texas nights, smooth Texas charm and dangerously sexy cowboys? CRYSTAL CREEK!

This March, join us for a year in Crystal Creek...where power and influence live in the land, and in the hands of one family determined to nourish old Texas fortunes and to forge new Texas futures.

CRYSTAL CREEK reverberates with the exciting rhythm of Texas. Each story features the rugged individuals who live and love in the Lone Star State. And each one ends with the same invitation...

Y'ALL COME BACK...REAL SOON!

Watch for this exciting saga of a unique Texas family in March, wherever Harlequin Books are sold.

CC-G

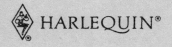

HARLEQUIN 💎 PRESENTS®

A Year
DOWN UNDER

In February, we will take you to Sydney, Australia, with
NO GENTLE SEDUCTION by Helen Bianchin,
Harlequin Presents #1527.

Lexi Harrison and Georg Nicolaos move in the right
circles. Lexi's a model and Georg is a wealthy Sydney
businessman. Life seems perfect... so why have they
agreed to a *pretend* engagement?

Share the adventure—and the romance—
of A Year Down Under!

Available this month in
A YEAR DOWN UNDER

HEART OF THE OUTBACK
by Emma Darcy
Harlequin Presents #1519
Wherever Harlequin books are sold.   YDU-J

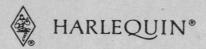
HARLEQUIN®

THE TAGGARTS OF TEXAS!

Harlequin's Ruth Jean Dale brings you
THE TAGGARTS OF TEXAS!

Those Taggart men—strong, sexy and hard to resist...

You've met Jesse James Taggart in FIREWORKS!
Harlequin Romance #3205 (July 1992)

And Trey Smith—he's THE RED-BLOODED YANKEE!
Harlequin Temptation #413 (October 1992)

Now meet Daniel Boone Taggart in SHOWDOWN!
Harlequin Romance #3242 (January 1993)

And finally the Taggarts who started it all—in LEGEND!
Harlequin Historical #168 (April 1993)

Read all the Taggart romances!
Meet all the Taggart men!

Available wherever Harlequin Books are sold.

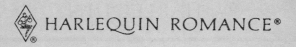

HARLEQUIN ROMANCE®

Norah Bloomfield's father is recovering from his heart attack, and her sisters are getting married. So Norah's feeling a bit unneeded these days, a bit left out....

Orchard Valley

And then a cantankerous "cowboy" called Rowdy Cassidy crashes into her life!

"The Orchard Valley trilogy features three delightful, spirited sisters and a trio of equally fascinating men. The stories are rich with the romance, warmth of heart and humor readers expect, and invariably receive, from Debbie Macomber."

—Linda Lael Miller

Don't miss the Orchard Valley trilogy by Debbie Macomber:

VALERIE   Harlequin Romance #3232 (November 1992)
STEPHANIE   Harlequin Romance #3239 (December 1992)
NORAH   Harlequin Romance #3244 (January 1993)

Look for the special cover flash on each book!

Available wherever Harlequin books are sold.   ORC-3